AVE
OF PO

AVENUE OF POPLARS

Elizabeth Daish

SEVERN SH HOUSE

This first world edition published in Great Britain 1998 by
SEVERN HOUSE PUBLISHERS LTD of
9–15 High Street, Sutton, Surrey SM1 1DF.
First published in the U.S.A. 1998 by
SEVERN HOUSE PUBLISHERS INC of
595 Madison Avenue, New York, N.Y. 10022.

British Library Cataloguing in Publication Data

Daish, Elizabeth
    Avenue of poplars
    I.   Title

    823.9'14 [F]

    ISBN 0 7278 5309 0

Typeset by Palimpsest Book Production Ltd,
Polmont, Stirlingshire, Scotland.
Printed and bound in Great Britain by
MPG Books Ltd, Bodmin, Cornwall.

Chapter One

"You see, I do remember," said Adrian Corder. He smiled and picked up a piece of charcoal and began to sketch a face. "I have you all in my rogues' gallery." He smiled. "Much more revealing than any photograph." He handed it to the dark-haired woman who sat on the window seat of his study and watched her face, as she took it, smiled enigmatically and handed it back.

"Out of date I'm afraid, Adrian. Haven't you heard? I married someone quite different." The Principal of the Faculty of Art at the university where Antonia Lambert had studied looked mildly surprised, as if the news didn't touch him but he did like to know what happened to people. She moved restlessly. "I know that everyone thought that Robert and me would marry, shack up together or at least have a torrid affair, but it just didn't happen."

"You mean that all that slacking off during your last term here was wasted? I recall a painting that you did at that time that was so good I forgave everything you had left undone and all your other failings and fought with the powers-that-be that you must not be suspended. I believed that you were in love, and being a romantic, I let it ride."

"Was it as close as that?" Antonia sighed and her dark eyes were dull. "I thought I had it made until I met Robert. He was so good that he made me feel inadequate. He could waste time and get away with it but I had to work for everything. I slacked off just to be with him even when we were usually with a lot of others, and to him I was just one of the pack."

"But that changed?" The grey eyes were shrewd. "After graduation, surely you went on meeting?"

Antonia got up from the slung leather seat and looked out of the window at a scene that she had tried to forget, then turned to face him, with unshed tears in her eyes. "It was a waste of time in more ways than one, Adrian. He didn't want me, *really* want me until we left here, and then it was too late. Before that he dated girls on a casual level, but not me, as if he knew . . ."

"That with you it would be special," Adrian suggested.

"That's what I wanted to think, and looking back it could have been like that, if only we'd had time."

"What went wrong?"

Antonia sat down again, adjusting her pale beige designer skirt instinctively. The only colour among the muted beige and creams of the well-cut clothes and the matching leather shoes and bag came from a brooch of rubies and pearls set high on the curve of her breast, conventional and expensive. The good light from the north window showed flawless skin and hands that were perhaps a little too thin, and her makeup was light, as if she dared not be anything but subdued and elegant. She smiled wryly. "Why talk about it now? I haven't mentioned Robert to anyone for ages, but coming back here, it seems like yesterday." She laughed more normally. "I didn't want to come here today but I'm glad now. Here, nothing has changed. I swear that you're wearing the same old jacket that we saw day after day when you dismissed our work as trash!"

"I do that even now," he admitted. "Hurt pride often produces some very inspired painting."

"Bastard," she said mildly, and he heard the other Antonia, who had racketted about the campus and laughed at life with an engaging and somehow innocent warmth, her gypsy skirts swinging over bare brown legs in the sun as she sketched outside, below the trees.

"Tell me," he suggested gently. "From my viewpoint I saw two people who were made for each other, and when he woke up to the fact that you are what you are, Robert did love you. He wasn't just lusting after another student; he loved you."

"I thought so," she said, in a low voice. "That's why we didn't sleep together." She watched Adrian's calm bend ever so slightly, and she smiled. "No, we never made love or we would not have been able to do what we had promised to other people. It would have been impossible to live apart for even a day." Her fingers twined round the soft leather strap of her purse and it snapped. "At least that's what I believed." She sounded tired.

"You had other commitments?"

"Robert's parents had promised to send him to America for a few months after graduation. He knew that they couldn't really afford it but were eager to give him one big opportunity to break into the art world there; to make contacts. You know." She shrugged. "My commitment was simple. My cousin has a hip condition. Nothing much wrong now that impedes her progress, but after a childhood of surgery and remedial therapy she thinks that she looks like a monster and needs a friendly face around to tell her she's great. I'd promised to take her with four of us, back-packing in Greece. Island-hopping was the in thing and she was over the moon, so I couldn't let her down."

"Sounds a good holiday," he said.

Antonia opened and shut her purse. "It was at first. Michaela managed well and even forgot that she walked with a limp, and the Greek boys found her attractive." She paused, then decided that she must tell Adrian more. It was a relief to find anyone with whom she felt at home. That was the trouble, she really did feel at home again.

Adrian grinned. "C'mon now, Antonia. You know I'm a cagey sod who can keep a confidence intact. Christ, I've had enough tears shed in this room and never breathed a word."

She nodded. "I was glad to get away so that Robert and I would have a breathing space. It was getting too heavy and I wanted to know if his feelings would last over a few months apart. When we came back we were to be married, if we both felt the same. I needed to know, Adrian! I've always been scared of casual sex, due, I suppose, to a very inhibited family background with no brothers, and an all girls' school. A lot did sleep around but fewer than most people know, and I had very good friends who just wanted to work and have fun." She looked down as if puzzled that her Hermes scarf could be so crumpled and twisted. "There was only Robert for me." "Robert did love you," he insisted. "So I thought." Her tone was bitter. "We moved about in Greece while he was in America and letters went astray or didn't catch up with us. There are far fewer postes restantes in Greece than you'd believe true! And Robert travelled a lot, too. He wrote that a group from this university had joined him at one point and they had hired a Land Rover and stayed together for economy until they got to the deep South." She laughed but without humour. "Remember Judith Morse? She was one of the party and she used to follow Robert about like a pet lamb, all boobs and dewy eyes. I know she wanted to sleep with him but she didn't seem his type and I never thought she'd have a chance with him."

"I don't believe it! Judith was pure watercolour and draped windows and vases. What could she find to paint in Maryland or Mexico?"

"Robert? Or just carry his paints and easel? She could afford to waste time and money and I can't believe that she went there by coincidence."

"Little mice do wriggle into the places where they can find the cheese," Adrian agreed.

"He married her," Antonia said and the dark hair fell over her face as it had done long ago, when she was in

5

trouble with her tutors. She pushed it back impatiently and the gesture brought a light to the eyes of the man watching her. He recalled that she had been a good student until she became obsessed with Robert Blackberne. "I heard nothing from Robert for about a month, although the others seemed to get mail when we were settled in Ithaca for a while and I wrote at least twice a week to him; then I had a short and rather battered note saying that he understood I was having far too good a time to bother with him, so we'd better stop writing, and that he was going on to South America and possibly to Australia."

"Could he afford that?"

"Judith could," she replied grimly. "And Oz was as far away as she could take him."

"And you? What did you do?" Adrian asked.

"You might not have met him, but he was here. Marcel Lambert, a Frenchman, married me. He was doing post-graduate geology here for a term or two. Very bright, with two degrees behind him; he left to work for a big consortium. I met him here a few times but never really took to him, then he turned up in Greece, having looked at volcanic rocks in the earthquake area round Port Vathy."

"Another coincidence?"

Antonia looked startled. "Yes. Of course. I'm sure it was an accidental meeting, but he did hang about and tagged on to our lot. He knows very little about art but paid one of the girls to draw specimens of rock strata for him to add to his portfolio. They are good and he could sell them for quite a lot now as Lottie has made quite a name for herself drawing wild scenes and a bit of surrealism."

"I remember her. How long did he stay with you?"

Antonia thought back. "He seemed to be there for most of the time, and came with us, saying that he could find what he wanted anywhere we went." She smiled. " He did make himself useful as he spoke Greek and sorted out a few problems when urgent mail with money from home went astray. He had to send away reports and pictures, so while we toiled away in the shade over a sketch pad or two and a bottle of Domestica wine, he did the shopping and posted our mail. He also bought and paid for a lot of our food so we didn't want to lose him! It was a good time," she added, as if she had forgotten how good it was.

"Was that all he did?"

"No, he did serious work and wrote it up, sending it off with masses of photographs. He's a very good photographer. Marcel took a lot of photographs and even sold some to magazines; his contribution to art, he said." She looked away. "Some of the pictures were a bit iffy. He took one of Michaela when she was changing behind a rock and she was terribly angry as it showed her hip scar plainly. It took us a few days to get her back to a happy state again. He liked to take pictures to give to the locals too, usually with a girl smiling by the side of a local Adonis, as he said it built up a rapport. We certainly got good service in the tavernas, but I hated having strange Greek arms round my shoulders and garlic breath in my ear while Marcel took just one more for local colour."

"When did you marry him?"

"I think he married me," Antonia said carefully. "Marcel is a man of action and decision and gets his own way."

"Obviously you have everything that money can buy. What do you do with your time?" he asked.

"I teach a little, but my husband wants me to give it up and follow him around where he goes working, usually in some dreary desert or canyon where there are no trees. He also says that he hates the smell of turpentine, which limits my output!"

"Deserts can be fun," Adrian ventured.

"I'd be bored out of my mind. I hate geology and his business pals are a pain in the ass. Do you know, I found I like teaching? I never thought I would, but as I have come to the conclusion that I'm not a very good artist, I turned to that, following the adage that if you can do a thing, you do it; if you can't, you teach. There are exceptions," she admitted with a smile. "I envy your facility to draw."

"Well, that's a relief! I spend my life teaching." He saw her unhappiness and laughed. "You are too modest. You can paint and you have talent," he assured her.

"But no real spark. Be honest. You didn't choose one of my works to keep for exhibition after we graduated," she said, referring to the custom of the faculty to collect examples of the work of promising students as reference, to compare with the next year's batch, and also to check with later work if the artist progressed and became well known. It was rumoured that there was cynicism mixed with this flattering arrangement. Some students did become famous and the value of their work went up accordingly.

Adrian went to a cupboard and looked at the row of hanging covers. He moved several to one side and selected a picture encased in protective plastic film. Like all the rest, it had the name of the artist, the date and the year at university when it was painted. "You sent this to us after you left," he said. "It's very good. I mean *very* good."

She stared. The painting of an avenue of poplars was bathed in soft light as if the evening sun was still warm behind the trees. The swirl of leaves tinged with autumn reds and ochre was almost abstract and within the branches was the merest hint of a face. It was elusive and maybe just an illusion. Darker red leaves made a gentle carpet on the grass.

Antonia looked at it for a full minute before handing it back. "I didn't send it to you," she said. She walked to the window again and looked across at the line of trees beyond the cottages at the other side of the campus. Dappled light through the poplars fell on green grass and made it look like young, swaying corn.

"In my opinion it's the best thing you did here and I'd be interested to know if you progressed to even more sensitive work after you came back from Greece."

She moved about the room and he sat quite still, used to the restless frustration assailing students who knew what they wanted to achieve and yet could never find the edge of brilliance that was almost there, nearly on the canvas, yet infinitely remote.

She found it hard to speak, almost terrified by the depth of her sorrow and anger. How could Robert have done this? How could he have sent this picture to Adrian, knowing that the whole faculty would know that he had rejected everything about her? It was a completely ruthless and public announcement that they were finished.

"Looking back is painful," Adrian said gently, "but surely life is good now that you are married and I assume have got over your somewhat immature idol worship?"

"Was that what it was? I suppose you must be right. It's a shock to find this here, as I gave it to Robert just before I left for Greece that summer. We laughed about it and said we'd hang it in the sitting room of our first home together if we returned from our respective globe trottings unscathed."

"He was always a man of sudden temper but I'm sure he regretted it," Adrian said. "I showed it to no one; I thought you'd come back, hand in hand, to claim it."

"You do know Robert," she said, huskily. "But this was obviously what he really intended: a complete rejection."

"He doesn't have that mane of red hair for nothing," he agreed. "He couldn't do his dramatic landscapes without his supercharged *élan* and a complete disregard for other people's ideas. It all adds up to the Robert I remember, and I imagine that if he is hurt, he clears the canvas, so to speak, and tries to forget what happened in a fresh and absorbing subject."

"Like Judith? He did write to tell me they were getting married. He just wrote that. Quite final, and I was devastated."

"Is that when Marcel took over?"

"He was gentle and charming and very restrained, and showed his devotion in so many ways that I thought, what the hell! I'll marry him, and we were married as soon as we returned to England."

She shrugged. "I found out later that he wanted to know everything about me. Isn't that sweet? He'd read my letters and even my diary, with all the references to Robert, and he knew that Robert would never let me go unless he did something drastic. So my mail was intercepted and while we were in Greece he had the gall to send those pictures of me with the local boys to Robert, with an anonymous note to the effect that Antonia was sleeping with any Greek waiter she could find after dark. Exit my love."

"And Robert being the arrogant bugger I remember, he wiped you out of his life? What now?" He held up a hand. "Say nothing more if it hurts too much, but I feel that you have a lot buttoned up that should be told. I'm just a piece of furniture, or if you prefer, a confessional, remote but ready to hear. Antonia, trust me."

"If I act the perfect wife, all is well, but if I get lost in my work or mix with other artists, life gets difficult and he reminds me how much I depend on him. He made sure I got used to easy living."

"A pity. I assume he'd object if I asked you to take on a class in Normandy for two weeks for students studying French landscape?"

"You're joking!"

11

"Joking because I don't mean it, or joking because you couldn't go?" he asked quietly.

"Both." Her voice shook. "Damn you, Adrian! I should have refused to come here today." Her cheeks were pink with emotion and her eyes held more vigour than he had seen since she first sat on the leather chair. She relaxed and gave him a tentative half smile. "You really want me to do that?"

For a moment her eyes sparkled, and he could see again the lovely, rather fey smile that had enchanted more people than she realised, hidden as it had been in the puppy love she had for Robert Blackberne.

"Could you? Is it so impossible? When he comes back for you I can ask him, if that makes it easier."

"No, don't say anything to Marcel." She thought hard and then breathed in deeply, as if making a great decision. "When would this happen? Would it be soon? Marcel has to be away for several weeks, soon. We had a row over it as I refused to go and booked a few private pupils."

"Almost immediately. I'll be honest. You would be saving my life. I have a school fixed but no tutor. A bad case of crossed lines over dates, and by coincidence when I looked through the files to find a substitute I came across your name and wished that we hadn't lost touch. When you walked in today, I was delighted for many reasons, not least that you could get me out of a hole." He sensed her uncertainty and laughed. "It was the idea of Normandy poplars that made me think of you. You had an obsession with the ones on the campus and this would be a progression if you could bear to paint them again."

"It's been a dream of mine to go to Normandy to paint. Funny, it's so close to England and we travel all over the world, but never there, and I would hate to go with Marcel." She looked sad. "I doubt if I could make it."

A student brought in two paper cups of coffee. "Think about it while you drink that stuff," Adrian said, but he watched her as he pretended to read a paper. "Could you be ready by next Friday?" he asked, as if it was settled. She rummaged in her purse and frowned. "Give me a ring if you've forgotten your diary," he suggested.

"It isn't that. Do you happen to have a headache pill? Must be losing my grip; that's the second time in as many weeks that I've mislaid mine. I keep them in my bag and nine times out of ten I never use them, so I don't know quite when I lost them, but recently I've had a few headaches."

He opened a drawer and offered her a choice of tablets. She took the simple aspirin compound but raised her eyebrows at the other one.

"Not mine, I assure you, but some of the histrionics I face at times need something stronger. The drug scene here has died down, thank God, but there are fringes left and it's senseless to disregard it and hope it goes away." He locked the drawer firmly and pocketed the key.

Antonia swallowed two tablets and drank some coffee. "I wonder if I could go?" she whispered. "If Marcel is away he need never know. I could have any mail sent on by a neighbour and South America is a very, very long way off!"

"So far?" Adrian raised his shoulders in a curiously Levantine gesture for one who had generations of the British shires behind him. They shared a conspiratorial glance. "If at any time you decide to go it alone, I could provide you with plenty of these courses all year round. They are quite well paid but not over the top."

Antonia sat back in the leather chair and regarded him with serious detachment. "You are the very first person to hint at the possibility of me leaving Marcel. I remember you as being almost psychic, which makes you such a good principal. I ought to hate you for stirring me up, but I know that I can't go on living in a kind of luxurious limbo. I have to think of my future and find the strength to do so."

"Do you love Marcel? There must have been something."

"He can be everything a woman wants in every way when he's in the mood, but he's so jealous that a visit to a restaurant is fraught with accusations that I smiled at men at other tables, and if we dine with friends, mostly his, and I'm too silent, then that's not right, either." She sighed. "I suppose I'm weak, but I end up furious with him for being like that and furious with myself for taking it, but the idea of fighting with him is exhausting and rather frightening."

"Please go to Normandy, Antonia."

She glanced at the gold bangle that contained a small, exquisite watch. "I must fly! Marcel will be waiting for me at the Swan. It was wonderful seeing you, Adrian. Even Marcel urged me to come back while he met the representatives of the firm sending him to America." She laughed. "I think he wanted me to see the sordid life I might have had without him! That graffiti on the science block is really something! Little does he know that you have sown sedition in my mind, bless you." She paused by the door. "I'll give you a ring tomorrow." The telephone on the desk rang and Adrian put up a detaining hand. "Me?" she mouthed and waited.

"Yes," said Adrian, in the voice he adopted quite unconsciously to give the impression that he was an ageing and very aesthetic academic. "I persuaded her to have coffee with me. I do hope I haven't delayed you? Please blame me. It's so pleasant to talk to old students even if it makes me feel ancient." He grinned. "She's on her way down and should be with you in five minutes, if you'll wait in reception."

Antonia blew a kiss and laughed. "See what I mean? Back to the ball and chain."

She walked to the elevator and pressed the button. The badly scrubbed graffiti was vintage and she recognised one that Robert had splashed over the wall next to the office after a painful interview with Adrian. The sooner I get out of here, the better, she decided. This whole visit was a dangerous mistake, and she smiled with an element of relief when she met Marcel in the lobby.

"Did you enjoy drinking muddy coffee again, darling?" he asked, ready to take a benevolent interest in her lapse back to student days, after hearing the dry tones of the principal.

"It brought back a lot of memories," she said and looked

away to hide them from his calculating eyes. "How did you get on?"

"I have to go sooner than I thought. In fact, I go to London tomorrow to meet the rest of the international team and then fly out next Thursday." She saw the relaxed expression on his handsome face and knew that he was very pleased with himself. She felt a flood of relief. "It's as well I decided that you couldn't go with me," he said. She hid a smile. After all his raging when she refused to accompany him on this trip, he was now firmly convinced that she was staying behind because he had forbidden her to go with him.

"Why couldn't you take me?"

"We have to go into very bad country. Only men are going this time. We have two female members but they will have to wait in the base camp and do the tests that we send back from the bores."

"What have they to say about that? I thought that they were particularly qualified to work on site?"

"I haven't told them yet. They'll do as they are told. Grainger and I are in overall charge of the excavation and they'll accept what we say."

"I suppose you buttered them up to think they'd be with you every inch of the way, protected by one handsome and strong Frenchman through darkest South America?"

He laughed, not annoyed by her sarcasm, or if he had noticed, taking it as a compliment. "Of course. You know me, my darling. I get what I want."

"Yes, I do know you." She shivered slightly and he handed

her into the car with solicitous care, his hand brushing her face in a caress, the thick gold ring cold on her cheek.

He drove well, in the certain knowledge that the car was opulent and expensive and in perfect order. At the lights, men envied the car and the woman in it, dressed as she was with easy elegance, her hair and skin perfect, but the women saw only the man with the deeply set dark eyes and beautiful features that gave an air of delicacy belied by the slightly cruel mouth.

"This means that I shall be away for longer, at least two months," he said.

"That's a long time." She sank back into the seat, her head resting on the tall leather-covered pads just out of range of his side vision. Two whole months! It was a wonderful prospect but she tried to sound sad to avoid the inevitable suspicions and questions.

"You'll miss me?"

"Of course." She laughed. "I'll have to submerge myself in work. I have lectures to prepare and I want to do some drawings of wild flowers before they fade. Last year I put it off until too late and found that the varieties I wanted were over before I could get them on paper."

The car sighed along the motorway and they stopped at a small and exclusive restaurant for a late lunch. As if to give weight to her comments, the banks by the hotel were covered with unsprayed clumps of milkmaid and campion, backed by frills of Queen Anne's lace.

"I could sketch a few here and take specimens with me," she suggested.

Marcel smiled indulgently. "I suppose I must spoil you a little now, but we'll have a good lunch first. Hungry?" He glanced at her as if he really wanted to know. "Who knows? You may have little appetite while I'm away."

"You think I might go off my food just because you have gone away?" She smiled at his vanity.

"It's possible," he said.

The dining room was cool and the clinically clean windows reflected fine silver and glassware on polished tables. Marcel looked about him with the air of one who knows that he can afford the best and has deference showered on him as if by divine right.

"At least it's cool in here," Antonia said. The headache threatened to surface again. She opened her handbag then shut it again when she remembered that she had no headache pills and had taken only two in Adrian's office, with no reserve.

"Could I have iced water?" she asked.

"No wine?" She shook her head. "No, perhaps not. It is warm," he said, and she eyed him sharply. Why was he being so considerate? At other times he might have lectured her on the insular attitude of the Anglo-Saxon to good wine and edible food, but now he ordered sparkling mineral water and suggested fruit juice instead of the creamy starters on the menu, and he offered no objection when she ordered plain beef salad and cheese.

The heat did little to impair his appetite and Antonia, watching him eat, saw a self-indulgent stranger. You have no idea of what could happen, she thought. Everything is going as you want it. You can see no time when I might want to end our marriage, no possibility that I would ever want to give up this lifestyle, and certainly no idea that I might find another man who could give me what I need. If only you knew that today, by insisting that I go back to the art department while you talked business, you have opened up a can of worms!

Memories that she had forced away as forbidden for so long now erupted and hurt like hell. Today I have reached a turning point, she decided. Has it only been two years? If I stay, will the next two years be the same? Days of pleasure mixed with nights of mingled release and frustration, depending on your mood, and whole weeks of deep depression bordering on fear when you are thwarted in any way?

"I'll go and pick some flowers," she said. "Take your time over coffee but I'll be ready when you call." That was the pattern, to amuse herself with his permission and come like an obedient hound when he whistled.

She picked the fragile-stemmed flowers and begged a plastic bag from a waiter. With cool damp moss they would retain their freshness for some time, but she'd have to work fast before they faded.

Strolling out to join her, Marcel watched her bending over the grassy bank and smiled. His hand touched the back of her neck and slid forward under the loose neckline of her shirt. As his fingers found her nipple, she froze, knowing that this was his sign that he expected her to be very receptive later. He turned her towards him and kissed her lightly. Her dark eyes were downcast and although he still smiled, he held her chin between vice-like fingers and made her look at him. "Is something wrong?" he asked.

"No, it's hot, that's all. I had a headache this morning but it's nearly gone now."

"Good. We need to make the most of the time left to us."

She could feel the warmth of his body and, with a sensation of self-disgust, she knew that her own passion would match his when they lay together that night.

He laughed as if reading her thoughts. "I have to leave you with memories. I have to set my seal on you so firmly that you can never forget me for a moment, my darling."

From an upper window a chambermaid sighed as she looked down at the couple who were so much in love.

The air was warm through the car window but with the air-conditioning and the windows closed, the car smelled of hot leather. From time to time, Marcel glanced at her, almost anxiously, and she couldn't recall a time when he had been so concerned over a simple headache. Perhaps he thinks I'll be off sex tonight, she thought.

As soon as they reached the low-roofed house and entered the cool hall, which every visitor said, with reliable monotony, looked as if it were straight from the pages of a glossy magazine, Antonia went to her bedroom and searched for her headache pills. At last, she settled for plain aspirin from the bathroom cabinet and decided it would have to do.

She went to the small drawer in her writing desk where she kept a small quantity of charcoal, separated in a cardboard container and wrapped in tissues to prevent the dust from soiling anything else in the drawer. She put a stick of charcoal on the desk by her sketch pad and then reached further into the drawer for the packet containing her contraceptive pills. It was easy to remember to take her pill each day when she went to the drawer to fetch a fresh piece of charcoal.

She recalled the time when she was first married and she carried the Pill casually in the pocket of her jeans or in her handbag and forgot to take them, resulting in a heart-lurching three days before her pregnancy test showed negative. Marcel had been adamant that children were in no way included in his next five-year plan and she had said nothing to him at the time, only too relieved to have nothing to report that would make him send her for an abortion. She had hidden them where she knew she must look daily and since then had always taken them carefully.

Marcel was reclining in the garden under a shady umbrella, the picture of a Frenchman satisfied after a gourmet lunch. The headache still niggled and Antonia wondered if the contraceptive pills were giving her a migraine. I can stop it while Marcel is away, she decided, and use a diaphragm for a while after he returns.

"How is your headache?" he asked.

"A little better. Have you seen my pills?" she asked him.

Marcel pushed his straw hat over his eyes. "Have you lost them?"

"I haven't seen them for some time. I thought I had two packets and they both seem to have vanished. You haven't been taking them, have you?"

He lifted the hat from one eye and grinned. "Funny girl," he said and replaced the hat. "Come and sit in the sun."

"I have to sketch these flowers. Would you like tea later?"

"Coffee at five," he ordered. "You haven't forgotten we have a barbecue date with the Rawlings tonight?"

"Christ!"

"No, he won't be there," said Marcel. "Just the Rawlings and their beautiful children and some other neighbours." She eyed him for signs of derision but found none. Marcel hated children, or so he said, and yet they seemed to be seeing more and more of the Rawlings' tribe. "Wear something pretty and be ready to leave by seven thirty."

Chapter Two

Antonia sat in a cool room with her flowers, in the suite that Marcel had designed for her when they were first married and where she could paint without the smell of a studio offending his sensitive nostrils. Even now, she seldom used oils when he was about the house but sketched in charcoal or ink. She pushed aside one of the loose silk smocks that looked good when she had to leave the studio and talk to a caller, but usually wore only when she could really work to her own satisfaction and he was away, took off her shirt, pulled on a cool cotton T-shirt and poured a glass of iced water from a vacuum flask.

She set the alarm for a quarter to five, knowing that once she became engrossed the time would fly, and Marcel would hate to be kept waiting for his coffee. The drawings came to life and she experienced a soothing tranquillity that came with satisfaction. The headache vanished and she began to accept that it was only when she was with Marcel that the migraine took over.

The alarm shrilled. "Damn!" she said, and sighed. There was so little time to do the things that really mattered to her. She made coffee and took it out on a tray. No thick pottery mugs here to be put on the grass and be held cradled between the hands while drinking, no cushions or rugs spread under a tree, but a continuation of the house, with a set table and almost formal chairs, fine silver and delicate cups and saucers. She had even changed back into the silk shirt and repaired her lipstick as if they expected visitors.

Marcel watched her pour the coffee and saw the colour in her usually pale cheeks and the sparkle in her eyes that was left over from the joy of working. He drank the coffee and followed her back to the house when she took the tray into the kitchen, and while she stacked the dishwasher and put the coffee away he leaned against the doorway. "I'd better have a shower," she said.

The soft splatter of warm water was comforting and her skin grew cool as she revelled in the one luxury that she did appreciate. The sensual slither of perfumed soap over her smooth skin was pleasure enough, but the soft folds of thick towels that held no memory of scratchy thin towels, washed in a launderette with jeans and sludgy coloured shirts, added to the illusion of being pampered, and her eyes grew soft and less defensive.

As if he knew the exact moment to find her at her most receptive, Marcel emerged from his own bathroom, still dripping, totally naked and very handsome. He took her into his arms and lifted her on to the day bed in his dressing room, letting her towels slide under them to take the drips from his body.

His mouth was delicate and teasing, finding every erogenous zone ever described and she tried to remain passive, fighting her own rising passion, knowing that afterwards, if she came to orgasm, he would find some way of humiliating her, as if that was an essential part of his enjoyment.

Her defence crumbled and she let the flood of passion rise and fall in ever increasing crescendoes until the light of the sun seemed to explode in her eyes and the world throbbed and pulsated on a tide of heartrending, sobbing release.

Marcel sat up and strapped on his watch while Antonia lay spent and passive, one hand clutching the towel as if to give her some kind of anchor, and to stem the pain of memory. "You'd better have another shower, and be quick," he said curtly. "Post-coital aroma on a woman isn't good at barbecues."

Antonia felt sick. To give in so easily was one thing, the duty of a wife maybe, but he made her feel like a whore, paid by time and dismissed with no residual tenderness as quickly as possible. The hot spray stung her shoulders and she turned the lever to cold, gasping but at least feeling alive as she washed away all traces of his lust.

As a gesture to the great outdoors, Marcel wore a deep red shirt open at the throat to reveal a gold chain, and stone-washed jeans, and Antonia felt like a clone of all the other women there, in designer jeans and soft check shirts that seemed to have been the choice of the whole of the stockbroker belt, the image of their prosperous community. Marcel parked carefully, avoiding the rosebed at the side of the drive, and went round to open the passenger door. He smiled. "Lovely house, but I prefer ours. They have no view and the terrace here is a bit public."

"They have no pool," Antonia said.

"Of course not. They daren't risk a tragedy with one of their children," he asserted.

Antonia raised a sceptical eyebrow. Really! Marcel might feel he had to be polite to the ghastly Rawlings' brats but he had said more than once that they deserved a fate far worse than drowning in a swimming pool.

The gas-fired barbecue was hot, with rare steaks and chops making subdued and discreet burblings and a long table loaded with salads and garlic bread waited for attention manned by two hired waiters. "Whatever happened to sausages?" she murmured and Marcel gave her a black look, then smiled. "Is that what you'd rather have? Shall I ask if they have any?"

"I was joking, Marcel. Leave it," she said shortly. "I'd better get a drink and circulate. It certainly smells good and I'm ravenous."

"Yes, have a word with Bruce. You haven't seen him for ages," Marcel said, pointing her in the direction of a neighbour who also happened to be their doctor.

Antonia was puzzled. First he was eager that she should have what she wanted to eat, however inconvenient, and now, he was actually suggesting that she might like to talk to a man who had in the past shown very plainly that he envied Marcel his wife and had made a few social calls when there was only Antonia at home.

"Hello there." Bruce Marden held up a glass. "What are you drinking?"

"A white wine spritzer with more soda than wine and lots of ice," she said.

"Good girl. It's much too hot for alcohol, that's if you're still drinking at all?"

"I'm hardly an alcoholic," she said and smiled. "I had iced water at lunch while Marcel had a half bottle, and one G and T before we came out."

"They seem to be eating. Let me queue for you and then we must have a long chat."

"I'll have steak and a large baked potato with a little tomato salad, please," she said and sat on a swinging couch under an awning, placing her suede duffle on the seat by her side to reserve it for Bruce.

"A whole steak?"

"A big one," she insisted. "And rare, if that's possible under all that burned stuff." She glanced across the lawn to where Marcel was talking earnestly with a colleague from the firm sponsoring the excavation. The light from a string of coloured electric bulbs showed his brown skin and strong white teeth as he laughed, and at least two women had brought chairs closer to his group just to watch him and try to catch his eye. He was very good-looking, she had to admit, and a dynamic lover, but she felt no sense of tenderness or belonging as she looked at him and wondered if she would ever feel jealous when at last he took a mistress, as he would, sooner or later.

"Success," Bruce said triumphantly. She laughed and took the plate and cutlery. "I snatched this lot from under the eyes of the vet, who also wanted rare steak but I told him that it was for a lady who needed iron."

"Liar," she said comfortably. It was easy to laugh with Bruce and she wished that they could be friends without Marcel suspecting that she wanted to hop into bed with him. Tonight Bruce wasn't even trying to flirt with her, but talked of friends he had who were artists, as if eager to entertain with no strings.

"My, you were hungry," he said at last, when she put the empty plate on the grass.

"Stay there," she ordered. "You haven't finished but I'll get some afters. What's it to be? Fruit salad or that wicked-looking chocolate thingy on the big dish? Cheese?"

"Fruit salad and cheese," he said. "And so should you. We mustn't put on weight, must we?"

"Speak for yourself." Antonia laughed and eyed his burgeoning paunch with malice. "I never put on an ounce."

She returned with a large helping of chocolate gateau with cream, and a dish of fruit salad. "Woman, you are without mercy," Bruce said plaintively.

"Here. Have some of my cream," she offered. "I didn't bring cheese as my hands were full and I might want some too."

"I suppose I ought to ask the usual things," he said when

they were drinking coffee. "How are you, Antonia? And how do you feel about Marcel going away?"

"I'm fine," she said. "Marcel has been away before but not for so long. I have lots of work to do and classes to take, and to be frank, I can get much more done when I'm alone."

"I'll pop in from time to time to see that you are okay," he said and she looked at him sideways, wondering if he really had forgotten that he fancied her. "I promised Marcel that I'd look after you, especially if he is delayed and is away for a long time."

"He suggested it?" She blinked, then smiled. "Well, you can begin now. I hate to mention this at a party as I know you hate talking shop, but can I look in to the surgery tomorrow? I needn't see you, particularly if you are busy, but I'd like a prescription for some more headache pills. The ones you gave me are very good but I've lost the last lot you wrote up for me. I don't often have headaches but just lately I seem to have a slight migraine that doesn't go away with aspirin."

"I'll leave a prescription for you." He looked at her knowingly. "But at least you don't need the other one. The Pill."

"What do you mean?" But she knew what he meant. Even his eyebrows were inverted commas.

"Come on, Antonia, don't be coy! Marcel said that he'd persuaded you to throw out the contraceptive pills and hopes you'll be pregnant before he leaves for South America."

She turned away, not permitting herself to speak. So that's why she couldn't find her headache pills! As far as Marcel knew, she still carried them in her purse and they were in blister packs similar to the Pill. It was evident that he thought he'd thrown out three weeks' supply, had made love to her at least twice before she could get more, and would now insist that she took no precautions before he left, assuming it was too late in any case.

"I don't feel pregnant, so you needn't bother with me except for the tablets, Bruce," she managed to say. "I'd better have a word with our hostess, I suppose. See you later."

She went to the bar and drank two large glasses of fizzy wine masquerading as champagne to fortify herself, then found Marcel who was playing boule at the side of the lawn. "We'll have to make a sand path and play this," he said. "I used to play it at home in France. Try it, Antonia."

"Now, in my condition?" she said dryly, and he looked embarrassed for just a second, then laughed. "Bruce seems to think I might be pregnant," she went on, watching his face.

"He does?" The deep-set eyes radiated triumph and pleasure. "Surprise, surprise!"

"And I seem to be the last to know," she said, flatly. "Why, Marcel?"

"It's time you settled down. Just lately you've been restless and all this teaching is quite ridiculous. I decided that it was time we started a family to keep you fully occupied and so we shall."

"I happen to believe that a woman has a right to decide what she does with her own body," Antonia began.

"A load of leftish university crap," he said calmly.

"*We* didn't decide this, *you* did, without a word to me. I thought that having children was a shared experience. Even animals can accept or reject partners when it comes to procreation. It should be something entered into tenderly, with mutual longing, not foisted on a woman as a trap to keep her in her place, wherever you think that might be!" Her eyes were over-bright as the wine hit her.

"You never look pretty when you drink, darling. Sit in the car until I am ready to take you home," he ordered.

In the car, she curled up into a ball on the back seat. "I shall go to France," she murmured. "I shall go away and he can think I'm pregnant until I choose to say I'm not!"

Marcel found her asleep and covered her with a rug. He was delighted with the whole evening and felt that now he must make sure that Antonia had everything she needed so that he could have a beautiful child. It would be dark like him; marrying Antonia had made sense. She was perfect to be its mother as she also was dark with brown eyes, so that even if they split up later, the child would be dark and resemble him and no other person. It would be a boy. A son would be born after he returned from America and he would miss all the sordid aspects of morning sickness and early pregnancy, and return to a beautiful wife carrying his child with dignity.

Antonia switched on the light over the desk to check that the contraceptive pills were still there, and saw that she had more than enough to last until after Marcel left for South America. She heard him moving about in his study and was tempted to rush in and tell him that she was still taking the Pill, but the wine was losing its impact and she felt stone cold sober. Better to leave him in ignorance, she conjectured. It might even be amusing to see his face over the next few days and to know that for once he hadn't got what he wanted. As she made fresh coffee, she imagined the letter she might send him when he was far away and she was safe.

"Coffee?" she asked demurely, and handed a plate of almond biscuits to her husband.

"Thank you, and I think I'll take the coffee black," he said.

Silently, Antonia handed him the cup and sipped her own.

"You'll find plenty to do while I'm away," he said at last, slightly unnerved by her silence. He had braced himself for a fight that for once he wouldn't enjoy. She wasn't even angry, if her eyes told the truth; almost amused. "You'll be a beautiful mother," he added.

"You think so?"

"Buy what you need. I'll make a large deposit in your private account before I go, and of course call on Albert if you need anything urgently. He's up to date on all our banker's orders and other business and you can see to the everyday bills and Mrs Regan's wages." He paused, but Antonia seemed not to have heard. "If you need more help, just ask Albert and he'll vet any new maid that you require at interview, but I suppose the most important thing will be frequent checks with Bruce and a gynaecologist that he can recommend."

"I don't need a specialist," she said.

"Have a pregnancy test as soon as possible, just to confirm

what we already know, and then take it easy. Promise me that you'll look after yourself?" He went to her and held her gently, his eyes more tender than she had seen them since they married.

"I'll do that, if that's what you want, Marcel," she said.

"Give me a dark-haired son with a strong body and a good mind and you can have anything you want; anything. Do you remember when we were in Provence in the spring?" She nodded. "I saw a boy there who could have been mine as far as looks went, and suddenly I wanted a child."

"Why didn't you say?" Antonia looked sad. "I might have wanted one too. We might have shared the experience instead of making me feel like a surrogate mother."

"We can share it now, as soon as I return, and remember, Antonia, that it will make you unique and precious. You can ask for anything you desire."

"Even my freedom?" she asked, coldly.

His face hardened. "You shouldn't have said that." He regarded her as if assessing her future worth. "You'll never find such a soft berth with any other man, but yes, if that's what you want after the baby is born, and he is mine to keep, you can have even that."

"Thank you," she said and walked away, leaving the cups for Mrs Regan to clear in the morning. At the door, she stopped. "One thing, Marcel. I don't want everyone to know just yet, and you did say that I can do as I like while you are away? I might take a trip somewhere."

"Fine. Visit a girlfriend or take in a few castles. Gentle

33

exercise is beneficial and you need to keep your mind busy. They say that music gets through to the child in the womb, so play good music like Wagner and Bach, in case it influences him."

"Him? What if *he* turns out to be a blonde girl or a false alarm?"

Marcel seized her arm. "Never say that. Do you hear? As for a false alarm, we'll make quite sure that it is impossible."

"No, Marcel! Please, not now!" He forced her down on to the pale green Chinese silk rug and tore her jeans away. She lay passive and cold under his thrusting anger and at last he rolled away and she staggered up to her room. Bruises on her arms and thighs were as yet numb but she took a long hot bath and wondered if he was really mad. Three more days of this, she realised, knowing that he would make quite sure that she really couldn't escape pregnancy by taking her as often as he could in the time left. Three more days and then she could escape, at least for a while, and think out what her future could be.

She dreamed of Adrian and the trees that she had painted. If I hadn't gone back I might have done what Marcel wants and even had his child, she thought, and as soon as she was alone in the house the next day, she telephoned Adrian and accepted his offer. "Can I use your address for mail?" she asked. "My housekeeper needn't know I've gone to France and the fewer people who know, the better."

"That will delay mail from South America," Adrian said.

"News from the excavations might take ages in any case,"

Antonia replied. "A day or so will make no difference and I'll be back within three weeks."

"I'm very glad you decided to go," he said.

"I am, too. Bless you, Adrian, you old devil. You do know that you have disturbed my nice, quiet, boring life, don't you?"

He chuckled and gave her details of what plane to catch and told her that her ticket would be at the airport. "You'll have a mixed bunch of punters," he said, "but it should have its moments. Leave the details of bods on seats and names to be registered to the courier and have fun. Just *be* there."

"What a lot of luggage," Mrs Regan said as she stood with Antonia and watched the hired car drive away to the airport.

"That's a small part. The equipment and tents and mosquito nets went by sea earlier," Antonia said. "Marcel always takes a lot of clothes and some canned food for his own use in case the local cuisine is a bit iffy. He had his jabs a while ago and has taken a very comprehensive medicine chest that our GP set up for emergencies." She laughed softly. "Everything but a pregnancy test kit," she said.

"Oh, you are awful, Mrs Lambert. Now, what do you want to pack if you're going away? Back to your old college, isn't it?" Her dark eyes took in every detail as Antonia pulled clothes from the closet. She looked enviously at the lovely dresses and skirts and hoped that Mrs Lambert would get a sudden rush of blood to the brain and discard some in her direction, as she did from time to time.

Antonia pulled a large squashy bag from the back of the

cupboard. It would contain all she needed, and the visit to France was going to be rather like a visit to the university, with little need for good clothes or formal dresses and suits. Absentmindedly, she peeled away the sticker that told the world that the bag had been to Ithaca, and found a pile of cotton shirts and a skirt she had forgotten, and would never wear now with Marcel. It was full and brightly coloured, with flowers and leaves and vivid patterns and a hint of the bohemian life they'd lived in the Islands.

"I'd forgotten that," she said.

"Not really you, Mrs Lambert," Maureen Regan said dismissively. "I wonder your husband hasn't made you throw it away. He's got such good taste."

"Just the thing for the campus," Antonia said and rolled it up ready to pack, with jeans and sweaters and one or two cotton sundresses. She found leather thonged sandals and a pair of faded espadrilles and gave Mrs Regan a dress that she disliked, which Marcus had chosen.

"Lucky for me we're the same size," Maureen said complacently. She glanced at Antonia with a conspiratorial smile. "I won't forget that you told me never to wear them when Mr Lambert is here. I keep all your lovely things for my days off and holidays."

"When I come back, we'll clean out the other wardrobe; I really must get rid of some more clothes," Antonia said. "Look after the house while I'm away and you know what needs doing." She saw that the hint of more goodies had won Mrs Regan's complete loyalty for the next week or so, and she had no idea of where Antonia would be during that time.

"Staying with the headmaster, aren't you?" she asked.

"Nothing so civilised," Antonia said, as if she hated the idea. "I have to be in charge of some students and he will only be there to see that all goes well and take in my letters if you have any to send on." She looked at the clock. "Make some coffee, there's a dear," she said, and as soon as the bright inquisitive eyes had gone she packed her passport and a bundle of French francs. For travelling, she wore a simple linen suit and took a large straw hat, smart enough if she saw someone she knew at the airport but muted enough to make no impression on the students other than that she was their tutor, and in charge.

Chapter Three

"Jeez! It's hot," Sam Bradfield said, as he sipped the coffee provided for the students assembled at the airport in the hope that the organiser could keep them together until they had to go through passport control. He looked round for a likely source of cold beer, but apart from the coffee bar the long corridor had nothing but directions to exits, currency exchanges and toilets.

The courier was twittering again as one after another of her charges escaped and it was nearly boarding time. "It's all very difficult," she said when Sam grumbled that they were late. "I hardly know who is in your group, as there have been several cancellations and other people taking the spare places, which messes up the name list. I don't even know the name of the tutor, but was told that she would pick up her ticket and join you on the plane." She looked worried. "Don't go away," she begged. "I must see what the pottery group is doing. My firm organises all these sessions and I have to make sure you all get on the plane."

"We going to have potters too?"

"No, Mr . . . er . . . Bradfield, they will stay at another villa a few miles away. You are landscapes."

"That's all I need! When I was told about this course, I took it to be a life class. I thought it could be a lot of fun, and now I find, too late, that I have to paint landscapes! Just wait until I see that leisure clerk again. He didn't say what the course was, but he winked and said something about artists' models and *la belle France*." Sam looked aggrieved. "He's paid to suggest interesting things to do when a guy hasn't enough leave to go back to the States, but needs a break."

"You don't paint landscapes?" The courier looked tired.

"Not on your sweet life. No, I don't paint landscapes, and from the map I can't see that the nightlife is all that hot where we're going."

"I'm afraid you should have checked, Mr Bradfield. This is a serious organisation for cultural pursuits and we have chosen some of the most lovely rural places for the courses."

"Jeez! Really no life classes?"

"Afraid not." She turned away to count her flock, and Sam surveyed the group with disgust. They looked like a lot of stiff-backed Brits bent on Art with a capital A. No fun by the look of them. Two women over forty with one giggle between them were obviously housewives let off the family leash for two weeks.

"Just like back home," he sighed. He recalled similar groups in the States, who lapped up everything to do with art and literature or architecture. Staying with dull colleagues in Scotland, on leave from the drilling rig, had been the pits, and when it was suggested, as he said he could paint a bit, that a course in France might suit him, he'd jumped at it.

He ignored the fleeting and timid smile offered by a girl with lank mousy hair who had listened when he sounded off at the courier. That, I can do without, he decided. There must be better talent somewhere.

The scrambled voice called them to their flight and he lost sight of the girl and the two women until they reached France and he found himself standing by the women at passport control.

"Isn't it exciting," one of the women said. "We heard you talking to the courier and we think we might be going to the same place."

Sam grinned, infected by their enthusiasm in spite of his disgust at the prospect of the next two weeks in some crummy joint away from everywhere.

"My name is Glenda and this is my sister Sara. We go to our local art classes in our home towns and this is the very first time we've been out of England."

"Is that so? I guess we are together in this group."

"You're American," Glenda said, as if making a great discovery. "I said to Sara, I bet he's American."

"Yes, ma'am, but I'm almost a limey. I work on the oil rigs in Scotland."

"There now!" The admiring looks were flattering and his ego blossomed. They might not be sexy, but they did admire him and he needed a boost.

They went through French customs and a notice held by another courier told them to assemble for transport at exit ten. The girl ticked off the names on the list and juggled with the names that had taken the place of the absentees, so that at least the numbers matched. A note handed to her said that one more A N Other would not be on the coach but would be joining the group later at the destination.

Satisfied, she chivvied the party out into the sunshine and then into the stifling heat of the coach while the luggage was loaded beneath them, and they sat in high humidity until the air conditioning gathered courage after the engine started. Sam noticed several other men on the coach and wondered if they were on the same course. If they were okay they might make up a poker school or go out looking for skirt. He wiped the sweat from his neck and cursed the cultural clerk, the heat and France. Piped music gave him an introduction to what coach drivers thought was the kind of music the tourists liked. Oh, boy! It has to get better, he thought, closed his eyes to shut out the glare and dozed, only fleetingly noticing that the pottery half of the passengers were deposited at a villa some miles before they reached the final destination and the coach finally stopped at a villa almost hidden among trees and flowering shrubs.

Gasps of pleaure from the two sisters made him really look at the house. Red hot geraniums scattered flowers and large flat leaves over low stone walls, but the dark green ivy round the lower windows of the house made the place look cool, and there were rattan chairs and tables in the shade of a huge tree. Inside the front door, the air was pleasant and stirred gently under a large ceiling fan, and a young man was already sorting out luggage when Sam arrived at the reception desk after the others had signed in.

Reception was cool, clean and simple, but the receptionist was not. "Monsieur?" said Jacqueline demurely, her doe-eyed look several years out of date – but who was studying fashion if it made a girl look like a knowing faun?

"Sam Bradfield," said Sam with enthusiasm. "Room *with* service, please."

"Pardon?"

"Forget it. Just get the name right. Call me Sam, baby. I'll see you later to find out what gives in the village."

"Monsieur?" said Jacqueline again. "I am Jacqueline and I welcome you to the hotel of my uncle." It was rehearsed and said slowly, but Sam found it quite enchanting. She consulted the list and smiled. "M Bradfield? *Numero huit*." She handed him the room keys and pushed a registration card over to him at the same time.

"*Qu'est que c'est?*" he said, and looked alarmed. "I speak no French. You must help me. I can't do this alone."

She smiled, showing small white teeth, her eyes dancing. "Monsieur Bradfield, here." She pointed and he wrote his name obediently. He pretended not to understand the rest of the card and she blushed in her efforts to speak to him and sort out the answers. Her halting English made him smile until Glenda came up behind him and took the form to finish it before handing it in with her own and Sara's.

"Spoilsport," he said.

"I can see Uncle glowering," she said severely. "You could get that poor girl into trouble. You wouldn't want that to happen, would you?"

"I wouldn't?" He looked at the swelling curves under the tight sweater. "Any time," he murmured. "Any time at all."

"Come on, you can't stay here with him watching." Glenda pulled him away, leading him relentlessly to the bar where the rest of the group were assembled. She chuckled. "I can see you getting into hot water," she said, and went to join Sara where they could sit in comfort but watch everyone coming into the bar or leaving it. From their glances and giggles, Sam knew that Sara was being treated to a highly exaggerated version of what had been said to the girl at the desk.

From their vantage point, the two woman could see everything and hear most of what was said across the room, and even when talking animatedly to each other, Sam knew that they could hear and digest what went on around them with all the practised skill of small town wives.

Sam sat on a bar stool by a potted palm and watched the door, hoping that Jacqueline would come through the doorway, but saw nothing of interest. He strolled over to Glenda and Sara.

"Don't you two ever let up?" he asked. "You've been yacketting as if you'd been apart for years and had a lot to catch up." He sounded envious and irritated, still touchy about being dragged away from the luscious bit at the desk.

"We have," said Sara. "We haven't been away without the rest of our families for years and it's wonderful." She smiled, and he saw glimpses of the pretty, rather breathless girl she must have been before marriage and children took their toll of her youth and innocence, and thickened her figure.

"You're both married?"

"Glenda lost her husband last year and since then has been nursing our mother." She turned to her sister with a look of affection. "You've been through a lot, haven't you, dear?"

Glenda shrugged. "I just want to forget about it. Don't imagine that I don't care or that it can be really forgotten, but after Brian's long illness and Mother dying last month, I felt I had to do something quite different, with people who had a common interest and something to *say*. Some ordinary package holidays consist of widows and unattached women doing nothing but sitting about moaning about their lot and doing damn all about it! Well, I want to paint and eat and rest, even if I waste my time here, and please myself for once in my life." She looked at Sara. "She needed a holiday too," she added.

Sam blinked at this sudden rush of vehement explanation. "I think you're right, ma'am. In a way I know how you feel, even if I haven't been bereaved." He saw Sara's scornful glance. "Gets pretty stale out there on the rig," he said. "Like being suspended from everything that normal guys are doing."

She giggled. "Like chatting up the girl outside?"

He grinned. "That, of course, but other things like not having anyone to talk to about books and art and living. I do have a serious side," he insisted.

"Surely you have a lot of spare time for that out there in the sea," Sara said.

"Time enough, but we play cards and listen to tapes, and

it all comes down to what the majority wants. It's a kind of brainwashing and it stays long after I go on leave, as if my mind has shrivelled and I can't take in more than poker and pop music and dirty jokes about women."

"I know how you feel," Glenda said with sympathy. "Do you know, I once smashed a tape that my son played over and over until I thought I'd go mad? Then I went to a big store and shut myself in a cabin where customers can listen to records that they might want to buy, and I just let Beethoven flow over me for half an hour until the assistant thought I'd died in there! I felt better after that and bought him a new tape, heaven help me!"

"I don't know why I came here," Sam said. "I'm not ready for culture. On the bus I looked round for a few guys to make a poker school, so you see how hooked I've gotten on the low life." He laughed and relaxed, half lying on a shabby but very comfortable settee. "I don't wanna paint grass. I think I'll stay here for two weeks and look at the view. Do you think she serves at the bar?"

"You came because you needed a change, as we did," Glenda said, with real warmth. "It's lovely to see so many different faces and to guess what they do in real life."

"So this isn't real life? No, you're not kidding."

"Do you see the girl over there with the beige sweater?" Sara said.

"The one with hair to match?"

"Don't be unkind. A lot of people have difficult hair. We can't all be blond American giants, you know," she said

45

severely. "She's a librarian studying in her spare time to take a degree in History of Art."

"Who told you that? You've been here the same time as I have and you know all that?"

"I asked on the bus when you were asleep," Sara said, calmly. "When I decided to come here with Glenda, I knew that I mustn't be shy and that I'd never get to know people if I didn't make the first move."

"Why her? Aren't there more interesting folk here at all?"

"She is interesting and shy, and Sara is being very brave to let herself go a little and talk to strangers," Glenda chipped in. "You see, Sam . . . you don't mind if I call you Sam? Sara's been stuck at home for so long that she's really pathologically shy, and now the children have left home she has forgotten how to be sociable. Most women have to make friends with parents of their children's friends for convenience on the car sharing runs, people on school committees and suchlike, that are only superficial relationships. They never really have the time or opportunity to choose their own friends, and when the committees end and the children have made other friends, there is a space that is not easy to fill after a lifetime of discussing school meals and muddy games clothes! Every time I rang her, she'd make some excuse not to come if it meant meeting strangers, and we live too far away from each other just to pop in for coffee."

"Glenda needed this holiday and wouldn't come without me so I made the effort and my husband said it was okay if Glenda needed me," Sara said eagerly. "He's always been thankful that he didn't have to have my mother living with us and he has a very soft spot for Glenda."

Glenda winked. "She really is doing me a good turn, Sam."

He smiled, thinking that Glenda was obviously the strong one who would surface anywhere like a bobbing cork after rough water.

"I had Mother to stay for a few weeks early on before she took to her bed, and she was very difficult," Sara went on. "I thought that Fred would leave me, he got so riled with her, and she drove away one of his best friends forever. Fred and Mother never did get on. We had more rows in a week than we'd had all our married life, and it took ages to get over it."

Glenda took a photograph from her purse, and handed it to Sam. "It's a tragedy that people get old and lose their sense of humour. They stop being the lovely people we once knew, and it's the daughters who have to suffer the bad temper and suspicions and moral blackmail. I keep this picture to remind me of what she was like when she was a real woman and not the awful old bitch I had to look after."

"Glenda! That's no way to speak of the dead!"

"I'm glad she is dead. She did her best to ruin the last few years I had with Brian before she came to live with me, and she hung about my neck to the last, going on hunger strike if I put her into a nursing home for a week or so to have a break, or having one of her 'turns' if she thought I wanted her to go to you and Fred," Glenda said firmly.

Sam looked at the picture. In it he saw two girls, giggling and looking at the camera. Glenda had been a real beauty before her face had hardened into sorrow when she was not laughing, and her body had become angular. Sara was plump even then, with a soft expression and a lot of humour in the wide eyes. "You look a real nice family," he said, handing back the photograph. The face of the older woman reminded him of his own mother and he suffered a fleeting pang of conscience that he had a letter to be written, long overdue. I'll write it here, he promised himself.

Glenda stood up. "I'm dying for a cup of tea," she said. "Nobody seems to be expecting anything of us and I need to find the loo and get that girl to bring us a tray – that is, if she knows about tea."

"There's a bog over there, unisex and very matey," Sam said. "I'll see about tea. It will be my pleasure," he assured her with a wicked grin. "I'll even help her make it."

"I can believe that," Sara said dryly.

"We'll wait here for it," Glenda said. "I haven't the energy to go to my room yet. I hope they put the right bags in the right rooms." She looked at her sister. "Go and ask that girl if she wants tea with us," she suggested, and Sara obediently crossed the room.

This could be me in a year or so if I don't try harder to make friends, Sara thought, as she stood before the girl sitting alone in the window seat. If anything happened to Fred, I'd be alone. I never thought of Brian dying until it happened, and I haven't Glenda's strength.

"The American has gone to find some tea," she said. "Would you like to join us?"

Jane Mellish smiled, and her face changed from tired mouse to a young delicate smoothness that made her much more attractive. She's even younger than I thought; Sara felt protective. "I didn't know that we could order tea," the girl said softly.

"Nor did I," Sara said and laughed. "I don't know anything about France. I expect you know much more than we do. To tell you the truth, if Glenda hadn't held on to my arm at the airport, I'd have run away home!"

"Really?" Jane gave a bubbling laugh. "That makes two of us. I was scared too, but someone began to talk to me about coming here and I dared not back out as my luggage disappeared at that moment into the back of the check-in area and I felt helpless." She thrust a hand through her long hair and smiled, then followed Sara back to the corner table.

"Sit down," Glenda said. "We live in hope about tea."

"Hello," Jane said. "Do you both paint very well?"

"Not really, but we enjoy it. We both go to classes and both picked up the brochure and we discussed it when I rang Sara," Glenda said.

"My tutor tells me to use a bigger canvas and to spread myself more," Sara said. "I doubt if I shall finish more than one small sketch here. It will take a time to choose what I want to draw; there must be dozens of lovely things and places here."

"You said you spoke to someone on the course?" Glenda asked. "Someone here?"

"No." Jane made a face. "That was one more reason for not daring to go home again. She's the tutor but she doesn't seem to have arrived yet. She wasn't on the coach as she said she was hiring a small car and would be here later."

"What's she like?" they asked together. "Not too strict I hope," added Sara.

"Very nice, and I think she's as scared as I am. Her name is Antonia Lambert and she teaches at home but this is the first time she's taken a course like this."

"A woman? I was told to expect a Professor Legrande, and then we heard that a substitute had to be found, due to unforeseen circumstances," Glenda said. "I hope she knows her stuff."

"I'd rather be told off in English than in a foreign language," Sara said.

"From what she said, Professor Legrande is very old and set in his ways and makes students paint the same subject as each other whatever they might want to do on their own," Jane said. "She met him at university when she was a student. She asked me what I thought we might prefer as she was new to the course, and she suggested that we have a talk about it as soon as possible to get different views."

"You seem to have got on well with her," Sara observed.

"It was a great relief. She is very pleasant and quite beautiful, and she said she wants us to enjoy the course and not to think we have to work all the time."

"Who is quite beautiful?" Jane looked behind her at the man who stood there. He was slender and probably not as tall as he appeared but he was graceful and small boned, which gave him height and proportion. The suntanned face was full of humour, the mouth lively and ready to smile, and Sara made a space for him in the growing circle of cane chairs.

"Our tutor," Jane said. "Have you met her?"

"Not yet. Do we know what is happening?" He accepted the seat offered and brought out a gold cigarette case which opened with a crisp flick, showing English and Turkish cigarettes and tiny black cheroots. He offered the case to the women.

"What fun! I haven't seen a case like that for years," Sara exclaimed. "It's like something out of a film." To her sister's intense embarrassment, she took a cheroot. "Now I feel like one of those artists from Montmartre that you read about back in the Moulin Rouge or wherever," she said as a sinewy hand held a small gold lighter steady for her. He offered the case to Jane who hesitated, blushed and then took a Turkish cigarette as if she too found this a new experience.

"I smoke little but when I do I like my tobacco not to be dried out and in a crumpled pack," he said. "I'm James Fahmi." His amused expression showed that he had seen the two sisters discussing everyone in the bar. "I suppose you want to know all about me, too?"

"Not if you've something to hide," Glenda said sweetly, and Jane blushed again, this time in apology for her new acquaintances.

James Fahmi laughed, and there was a glint of gold among the well-tended teeth. "I'm half English and half Egyptian," he said. "I live and work in London but my father is a doctor in Cairo, so my mother and the rest of my family are there too."

"Are you going to put us all to shame?" Glenda asked. "We are all such amateurs."

"I paint and sculpt a little," he said. Jane glanced at his short finger nails; the firm thumbs ended with well-developed mounts of Venus. Somewhere she'd read that this showed vigorous sexual desire, and she blushed again as if she had pried into his hidden nature. "I came here to study the light and to see if the old masters had put the truth on canvas, to enjoy good food and wines and to meet some people on business."

He looked from face to face, his mocking good humour daring them to ask questions. He's clever, Jane decided. He's really told us nothing but seems to have been very open and forthcoming. Everyone here will think they know about him and will never ask for more, while they will think I am hiding something as I am so shy. She sighed. If only I did have something interesting to tell them.

"Do you paint landscapes?" Sara asked.

"Sometimes. I have a penchant for tall trees." His glance slid over Jane's face and she had the sensation of being as compelling to a man as a fly on the wall. She stubbed out the cigarette, deciding that it was too scented and exotic for her.

A door swung noisily and Jacqueline appeared from the kitchen with Sam Bradfield close behind her. The girl put a large tray on a table by Sara and Sam put another with hot water jugs beside it. *"Merci beaucoup*, Jacqui," he said. The girl blushed, tossed back the thick blonde hair and walked away, conscious that every masculine eye was tracking her progress and every woman eyeing her with cynicism. The tight black skirt was no match for the turmoil of thrusting buttocks beneath it and the shiny belt restrained but promised a blossoming of soft waist and a release of bosom once it was free. Somewhere, she had read that a T-shirt tightly pushed down into a belt and no bra was the most daring and seductive way to dress, and the same magazine was probably responsible for the eye-shadow and the heavily applied lipstick that looked as if it was put on as finger paint, thought Jane with irritated amusement mixed with a kind of reluctant admiration.

"I never had much bust," Glenda said. "Doesn't all that get in the way?" But she saw how Sam touched the girl's shoulder in passing, and the tightening of the muscles round the eyes of the Anglo-Egyptian.

Two more women came into the bar but sat apart from the rest. "You can tell when people don't intend to mix," Glenda said. "They will keep to themselves all the time." Male voices from Reception indicated that there were more men on the course who had been to their rooms before coming down to the bar, and a dark-haired woman came and hesitated in the doorway. Jane moved forward and Glenda said, "I think that's our tutor."

Antonia Lambert smiled. It was good to be greeted in a strange place, even if it was only by the rather colourless girl she'd met at London Airport. It was stupid to feel so raw, as if she had never faced a class in her life, but her mouth felt dry as she walked over slowly to avoid appearing jerky. Her hands in the warm room felt cold, and her face was stiff with determined smiling.

"Hello, Jane," she said, and the girl smiled gratefully. "I hope my list tallies with the one at the airport," Antonia continued to the room at large. "There was a lot of confusion over who was coming, and I don't really know who to expect. There surely can't be four people named A N Other." Everyone laughed.

As Antonia stepped forward, clipboard in hand, Sam eyed her with interest. Married to an intellectual husband, he thought. Quite well-heeled by the cut of the skirt, and the sludgy-green cashmere cardigan that she draped over a chair was as expensive as the pleated silk. The general air of expensive hair care and makeup endorsed the impression. But beautiful, he decided. If anyone could break that shell.

"Do we line up for roll call?" he asked facetiously.

The dark eyes regarded him solemnly. All talk and no do, she thought, but attractive enough to avoid. "A good idea," she replied. "Suppose you all say who you are and I'll make a note and try to remember the names, but I warn you, I'm bad at that and you may all end up as er . . . ums."

"I'm Sam Bradfield from Scotland," he said, and a ripple of amusement greeted the very American accent.

Antonia smiled. "Not New Scotland, Nova Scotia?" she suggested.

"That's good! I like it," Sam said. "No, I really do work in Scotland on the oil rigs and I like to paint, or I did back home. I guess I'm a little rusty without practice but I hope to take back a good study or so. Any chance of life classes?"

"Only landscapes on this course. If I'd had more notice I could have arranged something." The serious reply quelled the glint in his eyes. "There will be plenty to interest you all, I promise." That's all I need, she thought. One lecher can be the death of any serious life class, and she decided that the list of possible models that Adrian had given her and which she had in her brief case would stay there.

Glenda and Sara gave their names and asked about equipment. "We were told that easels and paints would be provided, but to bring anything we liked to use and our own sketch pads."

"It's all here. The hotel is fairly small but the top floor has been made over to a studio, with everything we need. It's surprisingly good. I've been up there and I was very impressed. The garden can be used for sunbathing as well as painting and the beach is over there across the dunes."

"There doesn't seem to be a real village," Glenda said. "When we came here it all looked like ribbon development along the coast."

"Officially this is Blonville, but I agree. It's not really Blonville or even a suburb of Deauville, but the beach goes on for miles with none of the congestion of big resorts and yet we are near enough for trips to Cabourg or Deauville." She took the others' names and found herself two names short. One was a French student hitching from Paris and the other was the last anonymous person who had taken a place at short notice.

"Although there are two more to come, we'd better start or you'll go on the beach and get lazy," Antonia said firmly, and led them up to the studio. They laughed dutifully and followed her up the polished stairs to the room that spread across the whole top floor and had large windows. "I suggest that you take a locker each and put in it any equipment you want to borrow, with a basic ration of oils or acrylics. Take an easel from the pile and come to me for further supplies of turps and paints et cetera as you need them, and please take care of your brushes."

She sat at the big desk and opened her own files to freshen up for the first lecture, due to be given after the evening meal, but as more and more of the group interrupted her to ask questions she didn't get far. Some wanted maps of the surrounding countryside, and she decided that she ought to give them general information and the handouts of local knowledge on the leaflets supplied by the tourist board. It was with a sense of disbelief that she realised that it was time for dinner and she'd done no real work.

The dining room was large and opened on to a big lawn, badly yellowed by the summer sun and edged with reluctant flowers. The less regimented geraniums flourished with abandon on every wall and window ledge, with clumps of valerian in crevices, and Antonia wondered why the proprietor bothered with any other flowers. Wine, included in the price of the meal, arrived in huge carafes and it was already easy to see just who would take advantage of it. Three French families occupied small tables and looked at the artists with curiosity tinged with suspicion. A middle-aged man on his own sank into his seat behind a copy of *Paris Match* and ate solidly. Then he put a pencil mark carefully at the level of wine left in his bottle, rammed the cork home and glowered at the other diners before leaving for the bar.

"Do you think he sells vinegar?" Sara asked with a giggle. "Did you ever see such a sour face? You'd think the good food would make him smile."

The food was simple but appetising, with mackerel cooked in cream and a lamb stew fragrant with herbs. Tiny pots of *crème vanille* and cheese finished the meal and Antonia asked if coffee could be served in the lecture room.

Gradually it was unfolding. The faces, as yet still unfamiliar, were gaining identity, the atmosphere, helped by lashings of red wine, was relaxed and the interchange of ideas, as she outlined the possibilities of the course, was better than she expected. They made notes of the times of formal lectures and then asked about the place in which they found themselves.

Even Sam was being sensible. "Is there any transport we can use?"

"There's a beach buggy for fetching stores and fish from the boats which we can use when it isn't wanted here, so long as we top up the diesel. I have a car that can be used in emergencies, but apart from any special sights you want to see, I suggest that you remain here and paint. If you came all this way for the course, then use it. At home you can have good classes, including life classes, but this place has something you won't find in Edinburgh or London."

"Have we time to go to Deauville?" someone asked.

"Nothing is compulsory here, so it's up to you. Use your time well and take back pleasant memories of Normandy," she added with a smile.

"I shall paint this hotel," Sara said. "It's so French! I want to paint the wooden shutters and those geraniums. It couldn't be anywhere but France." She sighed. "I could stay here forever."

"That's a good idea, but some of you might prefer a seascape, or a country scene. Both are within walking distance of the hotel, or so I was told."

At last they had gone, leather sandals and canvas shoes slapping over the wooden stairs and the animated voices dying away. Antonia closed her files and put them in the desk. The two latecomers would arrive tomorrow, so their details could wait and she could brief them separately while the others put up easels and wondered if they had the courage to put paint on paper. It had been a long day and she knew she must be tired, but as she looked up at the sky to the west, through the high windows, she saw the afterglow of the heat and stars shining. The smell of turps and polish was homely and the feeling of rapport that she knew was rapidly becoming established with the class was good. For the first time in months she had no headache and no need to take any tablets, not even the Pill. I can sleep alone and have my body to myself, she thought.

The garden was dark and whispering. Antonia walked from the hotel along the lane and found the ground rising before her. From the slope she looked back and saw the outline of the hotel, heard the voice of Madame raised against the more reasonable tones of her husband and felt the cool breeze from the sea.

She was tired but not exhausted, but it was too late to walk over to the sea. She climbed just a little higher and above her was a murmur of leaves, a gleam of stars between slender branches, and for a moment she was back in the avenue at the university. The poplars of Normandy were no different but these held no memories.

"I have to paint them," she said. It would erase forever those other poplars and clear her mind for the decisions that had to be made for her future. She walked back, planning the next day so that she could have some time alone to paint, away from the group, then knew that they would follow her everywhere – she had agreed to teach them. I could stay on for a week alone, she thought with rising excitement. "I could stay forever," she told the stars and, at that moment, it seemed possible.

Chapter Four

The colours were bright and there was enough scarlet meridian left on the palette to paint the cloaks of a dozen bullfighters, but Sara was delighted with her efforts. Her cheeks matched the geraniums in the picture and a smudge of burnt umber gave her left eyebrow a surprised tilt, but what did it matter? The sun shone, there was no voice to demand socks and meals on time, or even to tell her to do something useful and not to waste her time.

She was glad she hadn't gone with Glenda and the others who wanted to paint a beach scene. The sun might not be as warm down by the water, and the breeze might leave a patina of sand on the paintings. Her tutor in England had been right. It was satisfying to use lots of colour and to cover a big area with bold sweeps.

The hotel slumbered except for the comforting sounds of food preparation in the kitchen beyond the hedge, the other students were scattered, doing what they wanted to do, and Sara was happy. She bent forward, her tongue creeping out while she added a sharp outline to the foliage of a lily in a large pottery trough, and Antonia smiled and nodded before walking on to see what Jane was doing.

It was pleasant under the shade, away from the parched grass and Antonia leaned against the tree. Jane's rough sketch of the hotel, a group of trees and some discarded earthenware pots showed an eye for composition and balance which promised well. Jane flung back her long hair and blushed at the unexpected praise as Antonia told her to make sure she finished it. Sun and fresh air were adding colour to the girl's cheeks and there were glints of gold in the long, usually slightly greasy hair that now dried in the soft breeze. The simple white blouse made her skin look lightly tanned and she sat easily on the wooden seat, relaxed and content.

"I'd better see if I can find some of the others," Antonia said. "They could be anywhere, as I told you all to choose where you wanted to be today, but you and Sara and the beach group are the only ones who said where that would be."

Everyone had been eager to gulp down coffee and croissants and get started this morning, and as she strolled round she found most of them, apart from Sam Bradfield and James Fahmi, and the boy who had arrived late last night, begging for coffee and dropping a large and dusty rucksack on the polished floor of Reception.

She nearly tripped over his recumbent body in the shade where he was half asleep. "Ah, there you are."

He opened one eye and stretched.

"Ready for work?"

He eyed her without favour and groaned.

"Come on," she persisted. "You had at least six hours sleep last night, and if you've been lying here since breakfast, you've had more than any of us."

He stood up, sending a wave of stale sweat into the warm air.

"Have a shower to cool down and get into something light," said Antonia.

"Do I stink?"

"A bit goaty," she admitted, smiling. "Lunch in an hour, so come down when you've showered and bring a pad. You haven't told me yet what you want to do."

"Will do, madame," he said.

"You sound very British, but with a name like Charles Renan and the fact that you are listed as a French student, where does that place you?"

"I did two years at Bradford and my third year in industry and go back to Bradford this autumn for finals. My grandmother is English and I've lived with her for the last year or so."

"So you aren't an art student?"

"Architecture," he replied. "With a special interest in Norman architecture. I thought I might pop over to Caen and Cabourg while I'm here and, would you believe, I never did get to see the Bayeaux Tapestry."

"So how do you think this course can help you?"

"I need a bit of help with technique. I do sketch but never as well as I want to do. It's useful when I want to keep a record of places, instantly recognisable and portable, and in places where they forbid cameras, it makes life easier."

"I'll do my best to help," Antonia promised. "Bring a pad down at lunchtime, which incidently is an hour from now," she reminded him again. "I may have a lot of free time today and tomorrow as the others seem to think they know it all and will come to me just for the formal tutorials until they hit a snag and cry for help."

He grinned and loped off towards the hotel entrance and Antonia wondered if she had time to make a preliminary sketch of the poplars. The noonday sun made short shadows and the trees seemed to stand in pools of dark water, with the topmost fringes of leaves making golden flames against the blue sky. Her pulse quickened. These poplars, in this bright light, were less sad, less evocative of lost love than those back at the campus, where she remembered them mostly against grey skies often heavy with rain.

I can use this time as therapy to make the catharsis complete. No more will there be memories and elusive faces among the leaves. I could be strong and free and happy, released from the past, not forever passive and yearning for what might have been. She added swift strokes and the formation took shape as she lost all sense of place and time.

"So you love tall trees too?" The scent of his Turkish cigarette made her turn as James Fahmi came close behind her.

"Where did you go?" she asked.

"I walked and found a stream with more of these trees about half a mile back from here." He held out a sketch pad and she was pleasantly surprised by the quality of his efforts.

"That's very good," she said, gathering up her own materials and putting them in the satchel she kept for that purpose. He smiled and matched his step to hers as they returned to the hotel. "If you can sketch like that why come to an open-ended course for amateurs?"

"My first intent was to come to look at Norman remains, as the early history of England and Norman France fascinates me; then I thought I could combine that with brushing up my art techniques and having my fingers rapped if I've got lazy." The scented smoke tickled her nose, and Antonia moved slightly away. "I'm a frustrated historian," he said.

"What do you do for a living?"

He stubbed out the cigarette against a wall and the dead ash fell among dry leaves. "My family have many business interests and it fell to my lot to take on those commitments."

"Is that what you wanted?"

"Do we ever get what we really want? Because I didn't train to be a doctor as my father wanted me to do, a lot has been taken for granted. If I was really the dutiful son I would marry and complete the illusion of strong family bonds at home and at work, but my English blood rebels at times against having a woman chosen for me."

"You could find someone who you could love and who would fit into the family picture."

"If that should happen, I have yet to discover her." He frowned. "I wonder why I'm telling you this? My intention was to sketch a little and wander about looking at churches, keeping myself aloof from everyone here." He smiled ruefully and she was aware of warmth behind the immaculate image. He lives behind a mask, she thought, and shivered, suddenly reminded of Marcel. But this man had a good mouth with laughter lines, and wide eyes.

"One of the drawbacks to being half English and half Egyptian is that I am a curious dichotomy of cold convention and sensuality." He regarded her with slightly narrowed eyes and even though she knew he was no threat to her emotions, she sensed a frisson of awareness that flashed between them for a second.

"That gets difficult?" she asked.

"Far too often," he admitted. "Would you believe that last night I wanted that painted little face in Reception?"

"If you hadn't, you'd have been in a minority of one among the entire male clientele of the hotel." She chuckled, and it was a sound that she had not indulged in for ages. "A wave of lust followed that unfortunate girl when she left the sitting room." He laughed. "Shall I wave a red flag if I see that look in your eyes?" she offered. I like him, she decided with surprise.

Of all the class, he had been the one with whom she felt most reserve last night when they talked, but she dismissed this now because it must have been that his looks reminded her of Marcel. She had felt caution almost amounting to fear when she saw his well-groomed insouciance.

"Would you?"

"You aren't serious?" He nodded. "With Sam here and

65

maybe the student who came last night, not to mention the gaggle of local lads who gathered in the bar to chat her up in her own language, I think you're safe, unless, of course, she makes a dead set at you." Her eyebrows shot up. "She has?"

"She followed me to the stream on the pretext of looking for eggs laid away from the roost, but she couldn't find even one!" Antonia laughed aloud and he gave a heavy sigh. "She came and stood by my side, with constant exclamations of admiration about my sketch, with that splendid bosom nearly resting on the paper."

"So, this afternoon, you will don the hairshirt and chastise the flesh to rid you of guilty thought?"

"This afternoon, I shall escape to Caen and refresh my mind with pure architecture, so if I appear to be slacking, be assured that I am still in pursuit of culture."

"Why Caen and not Cabourg, which was far less damaged in the war. So much of Caen was wiped out, and now most of it is reproduction, however well it's been done to look like the originals."

"I shall go there and become so absorbed that I shall miss dinner tonight here. I have an uncontrollable desire for *Tripe à la mode de Caen*." Antonia gave a faint shudder. "You don't like it? I can't tempt you to join me?" He had become boyish and carefree and she knew that they could be friends.

"Thankfully, I have to give a lecture and keep my class in order and I shall pray that we are not served with tripe in any shape or form. I tried it in the north just once, but never again. The only product of the region that I want to sample is calvados."

They went into the dim interior of the hotel. "Lunch in five minutes," Antonia warned. "If you don't appear by tonight, I'll rescue you from your room!"

"Safe, thank God," James whispered, and walked quickly to the stairs.

Sam was leaning over Reception with his seat twitching as he shifted from foot to foot to ease his tightening jeans. Jacqueline sorted out registration forms for the gendarme, who sipped pastis as he waited to check them. Her eyes were surrounded by rings of dark brown that had an oddly inflamed tinge, and the T-shirt was pulled even lower, thrust as it was into the tight, shiny belt. Her throat was encircled by a gilt chain from which a locket of baroque ugliness hung low into her cleavage, sliding out each time she bent over the desk. The result was a hypnotic attraction, as if the eye was compelled to follow a vertical metronome and to wonder if the locket would slide out, hover on the brink or stay trapped between the firm mounds of flesh. Sam was very bothered and Antonia took pity on him and broke the spell.

"Hurry up! Lunch in five minutes," she said.

"Did you ever see anything like that?" he asked reverently.

"Often on page three, and in most of the old masters. Maybe you too should have *Tripe à la mode de Caen.*"

"What's that?"

"A local delicacy guaranteed to cool the senses. No red meat, you see."

"What the hell are you talking about?" he said and ran up the stairs to wash before lunch.

The dining room buzzed with voices as all signs of the first reticence faded and they shared experiences and disasters. Sara was beginning to think her geraniums were a bit over the top but remained cheerful, and Glenda and her group admitted that they had done more walking and sitting in the sun than actually working. Others refused to show their work until it was finished. It all followed the pattern of similar classes but their shared interest made them a lighthearted and relaxed crowd.

Antonia listened to the babble as she ate her soup and was contented. Marcel was miles away and she was in an atmosphere that she loved and one that she had never had the time to enjoy at this level. The hotels that Marcel chose as suitable for their holidays, and the heavy opulence of his friends' houses, were all the same, like pictures from a brochure anywhere in the world. She had slept away afternoons in Spain, in Portugal, France and the Bahamas, in the same room, behind the same shutters, emerging to eat the same meals set to slightly different music – the only defining mark of the country in which she found herself – unless the management decided that featureless white noise was wanted, or pop if there were enough young people there.

A lark shrilled above the poplars and Antonia smiled. She recalled a cornfield where once she had flung herself under the shade of a lopsided stook and the larks had cut the day with ecstatic scythes of clarity. The pain of the sharp corn stubble was all a part of the joy and the dust on her mouth tasted of earth and pre-history. She broke more bread and enjoyed the sight of it, floating like brown icebergs on her soup. The freckles on her arms were showing darker and her face was full of sunshine after only one morning in the open.

After lunch, she changed into the simple peasant skirt that Marcel thought she'd thrown out when he told her to do so. She had bought it on impulse in Greece when he was changing currency, and when she saw it on the bed, she almost agreed with him that it was over-bright and slightly vulgar. Now, she felt more like the student she had been before Marcel took over, and the skirt looked good in the bright light.

Her room smelled strongly of expensive perfume and she wondered if she had forgotten to put the lid on properly or had spilled some, as she hadn't used it since yesterday. The stopper was firmly in place but a barely dry patch that had been wiped in a hurry showed on the chest of drawers. She smiled. It was a hazard that she encountered in many hotel bedrooms, and who could blame the girls who cleaned if they sampled expensive cosmetics that they could never afford to buy?

Whoever took it was welcome, she decided. It was too erotic and musky for the simple life, and she opened a spray of flower perfume that was light and subtle. The air was heavy with scent and she flung open the windows, suddenly reminded of Marcel.

"Coo-ee!" Sara waved and beckoned. A huge tray of coffee cups and pitchers was on the wooden table and the students were ready for the next informal lecture, under the trees. On the way down Antonia passed a despondent Jacqueline, dressed in a gaudy print dress and dangling earrings. Her shoes were high-heeled and tight, and heavy perfume followed her as she went to watch James Fahmi disappear in a hired car in the direction of Caen.

Charles Renan sniffed the air and grinned. He spoke to Jacqueline in rapid French as he went past her into the garden and she flushed angrily, her face sullen until Sam Bradfield came up behind her and slapped her on the tight seat of the dress. But even Sam deserted her to join the others for the lecture and she had to go and answer the telephone and resume her normal duties.

James Fahmi and another man, who had announced that he planned to be away all day sketching in Bayeux, were the only ones missing apart from Jane Mellish.

"Is Jane coming?" Antonia asked.

"She's borrowed the beach buggy and gone to Cabourg," Glenda said. "Madame asked if anyone wanted to go there as she wanted some stores fetched, so Jane said that today would be as convenient as any and she did want to see the town."

"I wish I'd known," said Charles. "I want to go there, too."

"Let me see what you can draw first," Antonia suggested. "You can put into practice any tips I give you and see if it helps. What have you seen here that you might like to sketch?"

"Apart from the bird in Reception?"

"Yes," said Antonia firmly.

"Ah, c'mon, Teach," Sam said. "If they have art classes

here on a regular basis, surely they have life classes. Don't you think she models? We'd pay her."

"No. Believe it or not, Jacqueline has been here for only three weeks. She lives in a village on the way to Rouen and this is her first job, as receptionist in her uncle's hotel where family can still keep an eye on her."

"Rouen? On the road to ruin more like, I'd say," Sara sniffed. "That girl is asking for it."

"Well, for the sake of the class, the future of the courses and the girl herself, I hope you leave her alone," Antonia said severely, looking directly at Sam and Charles, who had sat down together.

"Besides," Sara said with a sweetly malicious smile, "I doubt if either of you will get a look in. She's got eyes for only one man here. She doesn't want you."

"You don't miss a thing!" Sam said with disgust.

The lecture began and, as she illustrated several points she wanted to stress, Antonia felt an almost physical satisfaction in being in control and knowing that she was holding her audience. *If I could teach like this and choose my surroundings, with some term work in college, I could survive and be happy.*

One of the girls reminded her of someone with whom she had once shared a university house There had been eight of them, all from different faculties, but there had been few cross words, lots of laughter and mutual help, whether it was the exchange of clothes for special dates, food for unexpected visitors or shoulders to bedew with frustrated tears after bad exam results or broken love affairs. It had all gone into limbo for the past two years but now it was as if it was yesterday.

She set a project to study perspective and went from student to student, suggesting, correcting and talking, but sometimes just watching progress with a smile of encouragement. She had time for her own thoughts and increasingly they were with the past, before Marcel swept her away to cushioned but hostile boredom. Her headaches had vanished completely and she wondered if they had been partly caused by the Pill as well as by Marcel. It was a relief not to need protection and she had no intention of any one-night stands while she was in France.

A few of Marcel's friends had tried to lay her but she had resisted each time, less because of any deep-rooted moral sense than because she knew that all hell would descend on her if Marcel found out, and she dreaded any showdown with him. Besides, they were all out of the same mould, suave, rich and arrogant, and it would be like sleeping with Marcel, so she wasn't tempted.

The lark still sang and the bees among the broom were loud. That summer in her second year had been like this. Exams behind her and a few weeks hitching with Bess and a couple of Bess's cousins had taken them to Cornwall and the coast. The sea was cold and sand seemed to be a necessary addition to sandals and clothes. During the following winter she had found traces of it in her rucksack when she examined it before lending it to a friend.

Robert had been there, just once, when he and three other

men travelling by Land Rover had joined them on a beach to make a fire and cook food. They heated water in a galvanised bucket for coffee, and fried sausages and chips and opened four cans of beans. We had shrimps that we had caught during the day, she recalled. We waited until after the coffee was hot before we cooked them in the bucket, in sea water, and they were delicious. Robert wasn't aware of me then, but that day was heavenly. I had forgotten; or was it a pushing away of memories that were too precious to be picked over by Marcel and dropped into oblivion?

I'm really thinking again, as if I had opened a book long denied to me, she thought. I must compare that life with the one I have with Marcel and choose what to do. Maybe the old life was too spartan and I would miss all the comfort. Maybe I shall recall good times with Marcel if I leave him. Maybe I would be even more lonely than I am in his arms.

She smiled ruefully. Marcel would be furious when he knew that she wasn't pregnant.

"Is my effort as bad as that?" Sara asked. "I wish I could do portraits. You looked lovely just then, all sad and pensive."

Robert was good at portraits, but then he was good at most kinds of art. The cotton skirt flowed out in a bell as she sat on a log to see Glenda's attempt at windows, foreshortened. She had worn such a skirt on that camping holiday and he had sketched her on the beach after she put it over her bikini to stop the ever-pervading sand from making her thighs sore. One of the other men had draped wet seaweed over her hair and surrounded her with limpet shells in a pattern on the sand, but when he said she

73

was Ondine, Robert had smiled and said, no, Ondine had green eyes, and she had wished that she had green eyes. The men had argued, and Robert had conceded that she might be a dryad with brown eyes and hair, but not a water nymph.

I didn't love him then but I liked to look at him, and when we went back and met up again we went to concerts in the same group, we sat together if we went to the same local and attended classes together, with Judith hovering round him with a sweet smile.

"If you carry that line down like so, you will bring the eye to that point." Glenda sighed, and Antonia tried to be encouraging. "It's easy once you get the knack. Just try again lower down and it will come." She inspected the other drawings and decided that she could leave them and go to the beach to check the others, but first, she left a note on the empty reception desk, saying that she would be with the group on the beach until tea time, in case anyone wanted advice.

A large soft travelling bag lay on the hall floor with an anorak over it and she was halfway to the beach before she began to wonder if the last member of her party had arrived. It was too far now to go back in the heat, and as whoever it was had come late, two more hours would make little difference to their meeting. Another student hitching and saving on fares, she decided. No sense of timing on a course like this, where it didn't really matter, as no exams were involved.

The breeze lifted her hair as she topped the sand dune and saw the sea, glinting beyond the wet sand like a flat, calm mirror. The tide was well out, leaving a vast expanse of hard sandbank over which a horse and cart toiled with men digging for bait. Her students sat in the shade of an upturned boat and, from the sudden guilty rustling of paper as she approached, she knew that they were contemplating the other upturned boat that they said they wanted to draw, rather than working hard. The air was full of warmth and salt and tiny shrimps escaped along the diminishing rivulets to swim out on the tide.

She spent the next hour explaining the techniques required when drawing the curved lines of a clinkerbuilt boat, and told them that they had chosen a very difficult subject. She examined work, making changes here and there, and additions which revealed the curves and lines and still beauty of the keel. A child ran by, trailing seaweed, and she watched him go. Did she want a child? Was it essential to every woman's happiness to produce babies? She had many friends who were childless by choice and seemed very happy. She tried to imagine a son, with Marcel as the father, but the face wouldn't form in her imagination and she didn't want a petulant miniature of her husband.

The child ran to his smiling mother and flung himself into her arms, laughing, and she bent to lift him high. He was naked but for a tiny scrap of bathing trunks that left his buttocks bare and showed the dimples on his lower spine. A flood of longing made Antonia gasp and she was confused. If I wanted a child as I did just then for a minute, and know that I could love a child, why did I feel relieved that I wasn't pregnant?

She walked easily, her bare feet revelling in the sand. "Just carry on and show me what you've achieved later. I'll give a short talk over tea at five and we have dinner at eight tonight so that you can make the most of the light." They hardly saw her go, as they had become absorbed in their work, and she knew that nobody was really looking at her, so Antonia tucked the hem of her skirt into the waistband to prevent it getting wet.

What did it matter that she looked like a gypsy? She wanted to laugh and to run into the sun's path across the bay, with arms outflung, head back and lips parted. Her arms fell to her sides. To do that, there would have to be someone there, silhouetted against the slanting light, walking the golden path towards her.

Not Marcel, not one of the men who wanted her, not James Fahmi who had the touch of sensuality that could move her if she willed it. Certainly not Sam, who would look like an amiable ox ambling from the sunset and who lacked the finesse she would require from her dream lover.

She dared not think of the past again. She flipped a tuft of grass with her foot and it bent back, strong as wire and cut her toe. She sat on top of the dune and wiped the sand away, pressing the small bleeding point until it stopped, and saw Jacqueline with a huge basket over her arm, walking along to the boulangerie, wearing flat shoes and a sensible skirt now that there was nobody to impress. She shifted the basket to one hip and looked far more attractive than when she was over-dressed and sticky with makeup. Antonia smiled. Jacqueline, as she was now, would make a very good study: "'Girl of Calvados with basket'," she murmured.

The girl saw her and waved, then clambered up the dune

76

over the tussocks of coarse grass. "The bread, it is not there," she said. "I wait." She sat on the grass and turned her face to the sun, her lovely body relaxed and her legs bare. Antonia took up her pad and made a quick sketch. "I think the baker is open now, Jacqui," she said and tossed the sketch over to her.

"*Merde! Je ne suis comme ca!* Please, madame, will you do theese when I am . . . smart?"

Antonia shook her head. "You look very pretty like that and an artist prefers it to smart clothes."

"*Mais non*! I ask the others?"

"No!" Antonia's voice was sharp. "It is not permitted. The students come here to draw houses and the land, you understand?"

"But they can draw me if I want? If they want?" The smile told Antonia that she'd made a bad mistake. "I ask," Jacqueline said and swung the basket back on to her hip.

Three students were waiting for her advice and it was late before Antonia could go to her room and change out of her sandy skirt ready for tea and her next lecture. She picked out a simple cotton dress, wondering how she came to have so many expensive and unsuitable clothes with her. Even the linen suit that she had worn for the journey now looked too formal, and she knew that she ought to go into Caen to buy more cotton.

She hurried through the foyer and saw the back view of a man handing his completed registration card in at Reception. His red hair was well cut and his shoulders were good. He emanated an air of confidence. Antonia went through to the sitting room and someone handed her a cup of tea and offered a pastry that she took absentmindedly, although she knew it was too sticky and sweet for her taste. Red hair. Robert had red hair; a shaggy mop that flamed and moved restlessly as he walked.

"Has anyone seen the last student to arrive?" she asked. "I saw a case in the hall earlier and wondered if it was one of our bunch."

"He was looking for you, Antonia," said Sara. "I sent him to the beach but he came back saying that you looked very busy and he didn't like to disturb you."

"I saw no one," Antonia replied, with a creepy feeling that she had been watched. "What's he like? Another Charles? Or the man I saw at the desk, with red hair?"

"That's him," Sara said cheerfully. "You'll like him." She put down her cup. "I'll tell him that tea is being served here." Sara walked out and Antonia heard her voice. Sam filled the doorway and looked round for James Fahmi, shrugged when told he was away for the day and sat down on the window seat.

The space by the door was taken by another man, tall, well-built, with deep eyes under luxuriant eyebrows. A glossy beard accentuated rather than detracted from a firm cleft chin and the check shirt was fresh and workmanlike. He walked in and a half smile in his eyes showed them to be very bright and hazel green.

"Mrs Lambert, I presume," he said.

Antonia forced a smile that appeared to be frank, easy after all the practice she'd had, trying to be charming to

Marcel's boring friends, but she thought that everyone in the room must know how painfully her heart contracted.

"Hello," she said. "I think I remember you, but the last time I saw you, you had no beard. You must be Robert Blackberne."

He nodded. "That's right." He extended a hand and Antonia put her cup of tea in it, unwilling to touch him.

"What a surprise," she said, aware of the listening faces round her. "You'll have to be careful, everyone. Mr Blackberne is an artist of considerable standing and I can see absolutely no reason for him being here with us." She looked at him with careful composure. "I know that I can teach him nothing."

"I'm not really a student. I wanted somewhere to stay while I paint and this was suggested, but I promise not to get in your hair, Mrs Lambert. You'll hardly know that I am here." He drank the tea quickly and left the room after asking what time they gathered for dinner, and Antonia forced her mind back to perspectives of a different kind.

Chapter Five

Jane Mellish locked the anti-theft slot on the steering column
and put the key into her handbag. For her it was an achieve-
ment to drive a strange vehicle in France, on the wrong
side of the road, or so it seemed to her, and having no
guide to tell her where to park safely, which way to take
at the tiny roundabouts at the middle of each junction and
how to negotiate the huge traffic islands which had at least
four exits.

Cabourg was a mixture, not all of which she approved. The
spaces left after World War II, when bombed houses had
been demolished, were filled with brash modern shops and
apartments, ugly concrete ornaments and pretentious modern
sculpture, but sometimes among the dross she found old
buildings of charm and historical interest, retaining some of
the original peace, harmony and dignity.

The beach was some distance away from the carpark where
she left the beach buggy. She looked at the crude map that
Madame had drawn and saw that the shop that she had to visit

was in the same square and it would be simple to go there on the way back to the car. She bought a local guidebook and made sure that she had her bearings, as the dread of being lost haunted her whenever she was in a strange environment. Usually she found to her disgust that she wandered around in circles on the end of an invisible thread and saw only half of what she had come to see, but this guidebook was better than most and she found the house where Proust had written one volume of his great work. It was disappointing to find no remnant of atmosphere to equate with *Within a Budding Grove*.

The beach was crowded. Noisy and loud with the strident cries of French children. "I've got it wrong," she said and decided that she should have gone to Caen. She went to the shop to collect Madame's stores and staggered back in the heat to pack them in the buggy, wishing that she'd never left the peace and cool shade of the hotel and the opportunity to draw. She slammed the lid shut on the stores, approving of the uncompromising metal box bolted to the floor, which locked firmly to keep away thieves. It meant that she could leave the vehicle safely if she wanted to go on to Caen and find a carpark there.

First, she lingered over a *café filtre* in the cool and leafed through a guidebook of Caen which she bought together with postcards showing the various churches, deciding that it wasn't all that far away and would be only forty kilometres from the hotel after she left Caen. She made notes of the buildings she wanted to see, with names of streets and locations and approached Caen with a sense of anticipation. This time, she had more confidence.

The route led through leafy countryside to the bridge over the river Orme. A long, straight road, with good directions as she approached the city, made it easy to find the chateau and there was room to park and wander on foot. She bought a crêpe from a stall and ate it while she walked, as she didn't want to explore the shopping areas, and climbed as high as possible in the grounds of the chateau so that she could find and mark on her map all the places she wanted to visit.

The city looked beautiful and very old, but from her guidebook she saw how devastated the city had been during the war and how lovingly the whole place had been restored, conforming to the ancient architecture wherever possible. Glimpses of the shopping precinct showed massed banks of flowers growing in long stone troughs in the middle of each street, as if the city challenged anyone to say it wasn't a place of beauty now.

Exhilarated by the wide green spaces and neat gravel paths of the chateau, Jane walked slowly from one side to the other, seeing fresh views and making more notes. The guidebook was excellent and she was glad that she had bought it earlier in Cabourg, as she couldn't see any stall or shop where they were on sale.

From a seat, she looked over a tree-lined avenue and the country side beyond Caen and was suddenly aware that some-one was watching her. With no real visible sign of pleasure, as if she intruded into private property, James Fahmi inclined his head politely and smiled slightly. Jane blushed, not knowing if he wanted to speak to her or not.

"Lovely day," she said weakly.

"Very fine," he agreed, and his face relaxed into resigned humour. "Are you playing truant, too?"

"No, I'm on official business for Madame. She wanted something brought from Cabourg and I offered to help, as I wanted to see Cabourg."

"A bit off track for Cabourg, aren't you? Did you hire a car just for that?"

"I borrowed the beach buggy and went to Cabourg first to collect the stores, then came here. I've never driven one before and it's fun." Her eyes sparkled and he wondered if she could be over twenty years of age. Shades of the sixth form and head girl, he thought. "I just had to come here and see where Queen Matilda is buried," she added. "It's so exciting; really coming here and seeing it all."

He looked surprised. "I've been looking for it but haven't found it yet. I couldn't buy a guidebook as all the kiosks are shut for lunch and it's early closing day in Caen by the look of it."

"I bought mine earlier when I found that Cabourg was disappointing from my point of view. Very bright and crowds of people enjoying the sea, but not my scene," she said, as if apologising. She shrugged. "I hate crowds."

"So what have you found?"

"Over there is the church of St Pierre," she said. "Flamboyant Gothic and being restored. Not very old. Fourteenth to sixteenth century at most, but quite near to it is a couple of nice half-timbered houses which must be very old indeed." He sat beside her and eyed her as if seeing her afresh. "Over there to the south, I think that must be the Hotel de Ville. It makes a useful landmark but I don't want to see it." She smiled. "That's where I'm going," she said firmly, as if she was saving a treat for last. She pointed to a rather squat and nondescript building with a heavy gallery.

"That?" He gave an indulgent smile, his eyebrows mocking her.

"Yes." She blushed, sensing that he felt that she was over-enthusiastic about one of her pet subjects, and now she expected him to laugh at her and think her a blue-stocking. "That's the Abbaye Aux Dames built by William the Conqueror and Queen Matilda." She pushed back her long hair. "Most people pass it by, not knowing that inside all that hideous restoration lies some of the best Romanesque Norman architecture. It says in the guide that the choir, aisles and the vaulting were tenth century or so. Her tomb is in the middle of the choir, so it must be easy to spot." Her eyes shone and her cheeks were pink.

"Shall we go?" he asked solemnly.

"Oh, I didn't mean . . . I wasn't . . ."

"No, you didn't and you weren't," he said with a slow smile, "but if you'll permit a humble follower to bask in your hurriedly acquired knowledge I would be honoured, and you *do* have a guidebook."

"All right," she said awkwardly. "But it isn't hurriedly

acquired. I bought the guidebook to pinpoint everything, but I've been studying the period for ages. William must have been quite a character."

"In what way?"

"She was Matilda of Flanders when he asked for her hand in marriage but she refused him rather rudely, so he forced his way into the palace and dragged her across the room by her long plaits, kicking her as he went." She glanced at James Fahmi as if he must be laughing at her.

"And then, after such a gentle wooing, she couldn't resist him and they married in spite of the objections raised by the Pope that they were distant cousins."

"You knew!" she accused him, forgetting to be shy.

"It's my period too," he said, "but without you I wouldn't have found the Abbaye easily." They walked along the Rue des Chinoines and found the church. It was easy now to walk with him and to discuss the great semi-circular arches and the capitals typical of the period. She watched his sensitive hands caress the stone carvings and wondered how they would feel on a woman's skin.

"Will you stay and have dinner with me?" he asked.

"I can't," she said abruptly. "That is, I promised Madame I'd bring the stores back."

"Hell, Jane, you *are* on holiday." He wondered at his own disappointment.

"I'm sorry. It would have been nice."

"*Tripe à la mode de Caen*?" he suggested.

"Oh, *no*! I promised myself that I'd have that at some

time while I'm in Normandy, but I did promise to get back early."

He held her hand briefly after walking back to the buggy with her. "I have a few books back at the hotel that might interest you," he said formally. "We must discuss them."

"You'd better borrow this," she said and thrust the guidebook into his hands. "I'd love to talk some more about Caen." He watched her go, her fair hair streaming behind her as the buggy gathered speed. With proper care she could blossom, he thought, then turned away with her guidebook and forgot her completely.

Jane drove back, elated that she had seen the tomb, and oddly disturbed by the direct glance of the man who, to her, was the epitome of sophistication. I must do something about my hair, she thought, and wondered if she would go to Caen again.

Madame was effusive in her thanks and pressed a small bottle of calvados into Jane's unwilling hands. *"Mais oui, cherie,"* she insisted. *"Pour vous."* And what do I do with such firy spirit? Jane considered. It was too hot to drink anything stronger than wine diluted with mineral water and she'd heard that calvados was very potent, so she set it on her dressing table and walked down to the beach for a swim.

The tide was halfway back to the shore and it was easy to wade out and sit in a few inches of water until it came in further to make swimming more possible as it deepened. Her modest one piece was pale blue and one that she had bought for this holiday and not yet worn. She sat on the sand with the water covering her thighs, and watched the wavelets creep in to the shore until she was waist deep and cool.

Children shouted in the distance, made round, tall sandcastles by the incoming tide, gulls flew low to the dunes and there was space to breathe and to think cool thoughts, but Jane thought only of the man who had at last really seen her as a human being, when he held her hand on parting. She swam out, luxuriating in the soft waves. Her hair was saturated but it didn't matter. Nothing mattered now that she was free of her small confining apartment, her long hours of work at the library and her dull leisure time at home.

Splashing feet made her look towards the shore. Sam Bradfield and some others from the class ran through the shallows towards her. "We wondered where you had got to," Sara said. "We saw that the beach buggy was back but you disappeared." She adjusted a bright pink petal swimming cap and beamed. "Your hair is soaking. Want to borrow a cap? I have a spare back in my room."

"I never wear a cap," Jane said.

"Thank God for that," Sam shouted, laughing at Sara's confection. "C'mon, I'll race you all."

"Much too lazy," Jane said firmly. "I only came to get cool. I've been to Caen and it was very hot there."

"On your own?"

"Yes, I went to fetch stores for Madame from Cabourg then went on to Caen."

"I wish I'd known. I'd have come and kept you company," Sara said, and her sister smiled as she saw the change that the holiday had brought to her shy Sara, who now wallowed like a baby porpoise. "We could all hire a big car or a minibus and find the bright lights," she suggested.

"I went to look at old buildings," Jane said. Sara made a face. "Cabourg has plenty of amusements if that's what you like," Jane added.

"Might give it a whirl. It would do Glenda good to see a bit of life."

Sam floated on his back. "We can make our own amusement here," he said. "The boy who sees to the baggage plays the recorder and a cousin of his has an accordion and Madame said that some of the boys from the village think they are Elvis." He stood up in the shallow water and drew in his stomach, holding an imaginary partner while he gyrated and nearly fell over. "After dinner tonight when it's cool? Whaddya say?"

Jane kept quiet and hoped that they wouldn't also suggest bingo.

"Might be a giggle," Glenda said.

"Ask a few locals," Sam said. "Jacqui might have a friend or two who could come."

"All female, of course," Sara said. "You be careful, Sam. That girl is a tease if ever I saw one, but it's all show. She's very immature and young for her age."

"Ah, don't be like that, Sara. Everything about her is a come on." His eyes brightened with anticipation. "Make a bit of fun," he said.

Jane stepped over the yellow rim of the tide onto washed sand. She smoothed down her swimsuit to force excess water away and make it dry enough to put her skirt over it. Her wet hair went into a bunch which she tied back with ribbon, then sensed that everyone was looking at her. The slow grin on Sam's face and the sudden boldness in his eyes made her look down. She gasped and reached for her skirt, hastily wrapping it round her waist.

"My niece bought one like that," said Sara. "They go all transparent in the water. Shouldn't be allowed unless you're on a topless beach."

"I disagree," Sam drawled. "A little small but everything in the right place." Jane's cheeks flamed. "Very revealing," he went on, "and I swear that Jane's a natural blonde. There's proof."

She fled over the dunes and nearly fell on the coarse grass. Her breath came harsh and painful and she felt suddenly very cold. Tears of humiliation flowed down her cheeks and the drying fabric clung to every pore, making her look smoothly naked from the waist up where the skirt didn't cover her.

"What's wrong?" His voice gentle and concerned, James Fahmi steadied her as she swayed against the wall of the hotel. She saw his glance flicker over her breasts and then he looked away. "Come on," he said casually. "You're upset and cold." He threw his loose jacket round her shoulders and led her into the hotel. Jane clutched the jacket across her chest, breathing a little more steadily. "Up to your room and change," he ordered. "Then meet me in the sitting room in ten minutes." She shook her head, dumb with misery. "Very well, I shall wait by your door. I need some coffee and so do you, and I have no intention of waiting for it all day, so hurry up."

She braced herself to try to smile, calmed by his authoritarian voice. "I don't want coffee," she said. "I can't go down and face them now. I think I'll just pack and go home. I'm quite all right, thank you. I can manage," she said.

"Of course you are all right. There is nothing to upset you in appearing in a perfectly good swimsuit even if it shows your figure," he said deliberately. "Most girls of your age make for topless or nude beaches and show everything, enjoying the freedom, and nobody cares."

"I care," she whispered. "I could never do that." They were at her door and he saw that she was pale and shivering. He took her key and unlocked the door, pushing her gently inside and following her. She looked alarmed. "I shall be fine," she insisted. "I'll have a hot shower and change."

"First you must have something to drink. I see that you have some calvados."

"Madame gave it to me but I've never tasted it. Isn't it rather strong?"

"Just what you need." He took a glass tumbler from the table and opened the bottle. "Take it slowly because it *is* strong," he warned her, as she sipped then took a longer drink. A moment later she was scarlet-faced and choking. He took her firmly in his arms and patted her back as if burping a child and she gradually stopped coughing. "Silly girl, sip it." He held the glass for her, feeding her droplets of the firy liquid until warmth flooded through her and she was calm again, but the warmth came from the man who held her close more than from the calvados.

"Better?" he asked and released her abruptly, as if the intimate contact was no longer necessary for her, and for him, not wanted. He reached for the other glass and the bottle of calvados. "May I?"

"Of course." She made a movement of assent and sat heavily on the bed.

He poured a stiff tot of the apple liqueur of Normandy and his hand shook as he lifted the glass to his lips. He gasped slightly and set the empty glass down again, his smile forced. "You see, even hardened drinkers like me have to take it slowly or it catches the throat. A friend of mine says that drinking calvados is like having a torchlight procession marching down one's gullet." He was smiling easily now. "Get ready and we shall go down and meet the others, and I shall dare anyone to find it funny that you had this slightly unfortunate experience." She murmured a weak protest. "Hurry up, Jane. Do as I say."

He went out, closing her door behind him and Jane was aware of his strength and the sudden change from urbane Englishman to someone quite different. His father's people would be like that if anyone threatened the reputation of their women, she thought, and found the knowledge both disturbing and oddly comforting.

"You didn't stay in Caen for dinner," she said, as he led her downstairs. Her drying hair was light and fluffy and her eyes a deeper blue in her slowly tanning face. The clean skirt and modest blouse made her look even more like a sophomore, scrubbed ready for speech day, and her eyes were shy and wary.

"Just as well I couldn't find what I wanted," he said. "There were cafés serving what they said was the classic dish, but the one place where I hear that it is as it should be, do not serve it today. Instead of settling for something inferior, I booked a table for tomorrow and the dish will be cooked by a gourmet chef." Smiling, he squeezed her hand. "Now, *ma petite*, we face the dragons."

Jane laughed and when they joined the others nothing could have been more relaxed. Sam's leer died when he saw the steely glint in the other man's eyes and the women started to talk together until James ordered coffee for two and sat down with Jane. She looked at him gratefully but he was already appearing slightly bored. Charles and one of the other men looked in before going up to their rooms and Sara announced that she wanted to paint for an hour before dinner.

Jane took her sketch pad from her holdall and asked if anyone had seen Antonia. "I can't get on with this until she's seen it," she said. "I think I'll sit here and write up the notes about the places I saw today." She sat where she could see the garden and chewed the end of her pencil. When she looked up, James Fahmi had gone.

She moved to the window seat and looked out. Antonia was walking back to the the hotel, but she had lost the carefree lift to her head and the fluid movement of her body as she walked over the rough drive. She must be tired, Jane thought, teaching us all and having to tramp about trying to find us. She called and waved and Antonia smiled and hastened her steps.

"You look hot. Come in to the cool and have coffee or a cold drink," Jane suggested.

"I'd love a Coke," Antonia said, and Jane ran to the bar so that she would have it ready by the time Antonia came in by the front door. "Thanks, Jane, I needed that," she said. "I'm very hot." She smiled. "You look as fresh as a daisy. I'll finish this and take a shower. I had intended swimming but I just didn't get around to it today."

"I went swimming," Jane said and blushed. I might as well get it said, she thought, before Sam gives her his version. "I bought one of those suits that go transparent in sea water. I had no idea until I came out and you can imagine what happened."

"Was Sam there?" Jane nodded. "Never mind, he'll forget it as soon as he sees Jacqui." Antonia gave a laugh that held irritation. "I wish that girl had stayed at home. Charles hasn't even started any work, being too busy following her around, and as for Sam, well, he should know better, but he's organising a gig here tonight and Jacqui has to be seen to be believed!"

"I think I'll stay away."

"Please don't do that. I shall need moral support and someone to chat to our latest arrival." Her hand clutched the Coke bottle and her eyes grew darker.

"I haven't met him yet," Jane said. "You knew each other before you came here, didn't you?"

"We were at the same university. We both left and got married and I haven't seen him again until now." She drank slowly. "He's changed," she said softly. "That is, I've never seen him with a beard." She looked out at the garden. "He's had his hair cut, too."

"What does he paint?"

"Robert? Oh, most everything, but mainly portraits. He's very good."

"Why did he come here?" Jane smiled. "Unless he came to see you, of course."

"Me?" Antonia put a steadying hand to the Coke bottle that had nearly crashed to the floor. "He didn't know I was here. He expected to see Professor Legrande, who he met in America. His idea was to work independently of the class but to use the facilities here. He has no need of me to teach him. He was streets ahead of everyone in our year."

"Is that all right with you? You're in charge so I suppose you say what he can or cannot do," Jane said.

"He insists on staying, so he can do as he pleases," Antonia said shortly. Her voice was flat and dispirited as if she had argued and lost. "He will have meals here with us but work where he chooses, while I continue to give lectures without any interference from him."

"So, you think he'll be here this evening? You can talk over old times, Antonia. Did you marry a fellow student?"

"No, I married a businessman who I met on holiday after I graduated. He's in South America just now. Robert married a girl in our year but not an artist. Social sciences, I think."

"So you knew them both. That's nice," Jane said. She looked at her watch. "It's getting late. Do I have to change again? I don't dance so it doesn't really matter what I wear," she added a trifle wistfully. "No one will notice."

"You look younger than springtime," Antonia said with a catch in her voice. "Lucky girl, you still have your options." She rose from her chair and walked slowly away, looking sad, but there was no time for Jane to wonder at what her tutor was thinking.

Sam rushed through the room in hot pursuit of Jacqui, who squeaked with mock fear and shock. Jane stared. Jacqui wore a see-through shirt of patterned voile which made scars of colour on her shoulders and showed the heavily frilled bra beneath it. The bright blue skirt was slashed to the thigh and fishnet tights finished the apparition. Jane blinked and then laughed. There was certainly no need now to think that anyone recalled her embarrassment on the beach.

James Fahmi walked through on his way to the dining room, pausing to light a cigarette and so didn't notice her. Would he even remember her name in a week or so? She joined Sara and Glenda and found that she was hungry.

The Frenchman, who was still morosely alone, examined his bottle of wine with deep suspicion and poured out a bare half glass to which he added mineral water. "I wonder if he dances?" Sara said with a giggle. French families were already tucking into small shellfish and soup, and Jane ate unfamilar food that tasted good. James sat opposite her, two places away, but seemed absorbed in his baby clams and didn't look up. Jane watched him and tried to make out if he was really as stern as he now appeared to be or if the real James was the Englishman with the sweet smile.

"I love all this sea food," Glenda said. "Why don't we have fish like this at home? After all, we are only a few miles across the water and we must have it in our sea, too. We are going to Cabourg tomorrow for dinner," she went on. "Madame says that she isn't serving dinner here as she is going shopping with Jacqui. We can have a salad lunch here and eat later in the café down the road or go further out. She suggested a restaurant in Cabourg where they have crayfish and a cabaret. We can hire a car for six and another if enough people want to come."

"Sounds great. A good chance to see some more of the local talent without Jacqui breathing down my neck."

Charles regarded Sam with derision. "Who breathes down whose neck?"

"You can just take that look off your face, Charles. Jacqui really fancies me."

"*Je crois!*"

"What about you, Jane?" Sara asked. "You'll come with us? I have to take numbers now as the hire car people want to know soon. They want me to ring back early tomorrow."

Jane hesitated, unwilling to seem unfriendly but hating the whole idea of a knees-up in Cabourg with loud music and not being able to come away when she wanted to, as she would be tied to the time when the car left.

"Jane can't go," James Fahmi said calmly. "I have to pay my debts. She helped me to find some places of real interest in Caen and I owe her a dinner." He smiled as if being coldly polite. "We are going to Caen tomorrow evening." She gasped. "I managed to book a table," he said, as if she was fully aware of his plans.

"That's lovely," Jane said weakly.

"Oh, damn. That's two empty seats so far. I was sure that you would come, James," Sara said.

"I'm afraid that crayfish *à la mode de Cabourg* doesn't agree with me," he said solemnly.

"Poor you not to be able to eat crayfish," Sara said with sympathy. "You don't know what you're missing."

"I think I do, but I shall think of you while I eat tripe, and Jane shall keep me company," he said.

"That's tomorrow, but we still have tonight," Sam said. "I've thought about it and why don't we have a beach party? It will be less trouble for Madame, who is looking a bit sour about the noise we might make, and we can really spread ourselves and have fun. Whaddya say?"

"Jacqui is not really dressed for the beach," Antonia said. "Watch it, Sam! She's only a child."

"Me?" Sam looked hurt. "Would I do anything to her?"

"Chance would be a fine thing," Sara said. "She can run, even in those high heels, and you have rivals."

"I asked Andre to collect wood for a fire and gave him some dough to spend on a flagon of the local wine. My treat," he added expansively. "But you all have to join in. Anybody here sing?"

"Don't tell us that you do?" Charles said with a groan.

"Why not. They say back home that I sing Country real good."

"Great," Sara said. "I love wood fires and it's so warm that we might be able to swim in the moonlight."

There seemed to be no escape so Antonia went to fetch a rug and a sweater in case the night turned cold, and James Fahmi found himself lifting one end of the bench that Charles said would be needed on the dunes, and gradually the magic of the sea at night took over and they were all laughing, except Jacqui who found her skirt far too tight to sit in on the sand. She changed her shoes and brought out a shabby fur fabric duvet and hoped that she looked like Cleopatra reclining on a leopardskin.

Antonia looked round at the group trying to get a sea-damp log to catch light from the glowing heart of the fire, and noticed that Robert Blackberne was not among them. It was a relief and yet she waited, wondering where he went when he was away from the hotel and what he found to do each time he vanished in the small car. Apart from the first meeting, she had seen only glimpses of him leaving, and he never ate at the hotel, apart from having breakfast alone in his room. At least I can't accuse him of interference, she admitted ruefully. He is as anxious as I am not to meet again and none of the students seem to have got to know him or found out anything of interest.

The moon obediently hung high and bright and the music played by the local boys was surprisingly good. Wine raised the level of laughter and Charles and Sam plied Jacqui with wine, which she hated and refused, and salty biscuits that made her demand endless supplies of Coke and left her completely unresponsive to their efforts. She glanced at James Fahmi from time to time and wondered if the agony aunt in her favourite magazine would suggest ways of attracting a man who seemed to prefer to gaze into the fire rather than to look at her in all her finery. Surely the sight of Sam and Charles trying to win her attention was enough to make any man jealous, but he ignored everyone and seemed deep in serious thought.

Antonia heard a car arrive but could see nothing through the trees. She frowned. Would every sound make her think it was Robert coming back to the hotel? What did it matter? He was a ghost from the past and after a short time would return there to Judith – and what else? Had he a family now? Judith looked productive enough. Her heart contracted. Robert's children would be difficult, wild and completely beautiful. She threw a stick onto the fire and watched it burn.

A door banged but there was no other sound from the hotel; any noise was muffled by the dunes. Robert didn't appear, as she thought he might out of curiosity and his love of outdoor things. If he wanted to come he would do so and take no notice of me, she decided. Had Judith tamed him so much? As Marcel tamed me? She dribbled dry sand over her ankles and remembered another time, when the sand had been cool after dark and the fire on the beach had been the centre of another group, and she had watched a man's eyes, bright with the glow of youth, in a time of innocence.

The fire was dying to a red heart. Antonia stood up,

murmuring something about going back to the loo and Glenda smiled and nodded, expecting her to come back.

"I've never done this before," Sara said. "We didn't know what we were missing. When I get back, I want to buy a barbecue, Glenda, and when you come to stay we can have a party, and a bit of a sing-song."

"Keep my rug until you go back," Antonia said. "I may go to bed, so make sure it gets returned safely, but use it now."

"Don't go to bed!" Sara called, but Antonia just waved a languid hand, making no promise. It was late, she knew that sleep would be difficult and she had no sleeping pills. Nor did she want to sleep. The night was beautiful and it was better to walk in the air than to toss restlessly and wait for the dawn. She went into the hotel. Most of the lights were dimmed as a hint that service was non-existent and Madame and Monsieur had gone to bed. She took a long drink from the bottle of mineral water she kept by her bed and walked downstairs again into the garden.

The muted sounds from the party made her turn away to the grove of trees that she had been drawing. She could see the moon through the leaves as if through a filigree, but now small clouds brushed past the white light and made shadows, and she wanted to weep.

Chapter Six

"Oh, c'mon, the night's young," said Sam Bradfield. He stirred the dying embers of the beach fire and the flames lit the faces of a circle of sleepy villagers and artists. Jacqueline still reclined in what she hoped was a seductive pose and pouted when her efforts to attract James Fahmi had just the opposite effect. She sighed. Why was it easy to make Sam and Charles hang on every word she uttered, when James Fahmi avoided even glancing at her?

James stood up and stretched. "I'm going now," he said firmly, his slender body supple and slight against the dark of the beach. He turned to Jane. "I gave back the guidebook but now I think I would like to borrow it again. I want to look up something about L'Abbaye and check a date. Jane?" he said more loudly as she continued to sit on the sand and to look deep into the fire.

Jane started, confused that he should now bother to speak to her after ignoring her for hours and avoiding conversation with the others, as if he had something on his mind that upset him to the point of hidden anger.

"May I borrow the guidebook for Caen?" he asked again impatiently.

"Do you want it now?" she asked.

"If it isn't too much trouble," he said politely. "We could walk back together." His glance flickered over Jacqui who was now sitting up as if about to leave too, as soon as she saw that he wanted to go back.

"That's all right. I was about to leave now," Jane said, struggling to her feet with the ungainly grace of a netball captain. She put a hand on Sara's shoulder to steady herself. "Cramp in my toes from sitting so long," she said cheerfully, and hobbled after James.

Jacqui watched them go, and wished Jane to hell. She was unaware that her mascara had run badly after a wave of smoke had made her eyes water and she didn't hear Charles Renan tell her about it until he repeated himself and handed her a tissue. She snatched it furiously and rubbed the smudges from her cheeks, angry that it was Charles who had told her that she was less than beautiful, in the mocking way he spoke to her, but cheering up when Sam showed that he, at least, was impressed. Without her dark smudges she wondered if James might have been more attentive if he had stayed. *Zut*, we could have walked together, she thought wistfully.

Charles came closer and gave her a chocolate bar from England. She took it with bad grace, as she suspected that he was still laughing at her, but his eyes held the same expression that she had come to find in many mens' eyes. He broke off tiny pieces of chocolate and fed her as if she was a kitten and she found herself laughing. As his hands touched her face, she decided that he was nearly as attractive as the so-cold James Fahmi, for all his good looks and nice teeth. Charles murmured words of admiration in French, interspersed with phrases in English that she didn't understand but thought were more romantic.

Charles was enjoying himself. It was fun to call Jacqui a pretty little cow with no sense, in English, and see her lap up the misunderstood compliments. It was also good to think that he was putting that loud-mouthed American in his place, so he went on calling Jacqui a raving nympho, a silly cunt and a stupid little tramp, all in the tenderest tones. Silly bitch, he thought. She's like a dog wagging its tail with pleasure when it's called a dirty tyke in a fond voice.

He chuckled as Jacqui tried to memorise the words he used, wanting to recount to her friends the ultimate in English love talk, and he pulled her to her feet. She smoothed down the crumpled skirt that was completely wrong for the beach and carried her shoes. They walked back to the hotel barefooted and in the shadows he kissed her. She broke away as his hands began to wander over her body and Sam heard their laughter as Charles chased her back to the safety of the hotel and the room next door to her aunt and uncle where no man dared to follow.

Sam realised that he was nearly alone. The villagers and other students had wandered off as soon as all the wine had gone. Sara and Glenda were yawning and packing up their rush mats and cardigans. The fire was nearly out and what wood was left had not dried enough to use. Sam tossed a piece of damp bark into the fire and it sat there, smouldering blackly. "Damn!" he said. He had expected better of the evening, but Jacqui had eyes only for Fahmi until he left and then the tantalising little bitch had gone off with Charles. He staggered back along the path, more drunk than he knew and very depressed.

"There must be more to life than this," he muttered. The lights were going out all over the hotel, one bedroom after another showing dark. He saw Sara and Glenda go into the hall and disappear in the direction of the sitting room. Even they would have been better company than his own. The village boys had stared at him as if he was a strange animal and stayed only as long as the drink lasted, and now his own group had deserted him. If only Jacqui was on the beach now. He pictured her as she had been during the singing, when she had looked at him with admiration while he sang country and western, and she had sat there with that ridiculous transparent blouse just waiting to be torn off.

He went into the hotel and saw Jane Mellish coming downstairs with a book in her hand. "Hi!" he said, and smiled.

"Oh, hello. Is everyone back from the beach? I hope we didn't break it up. I have to give this to James," she said, vaguely unsure of the expression in Sam's eyes. Glenda was drinking hot chocolate made by the boy who had played the accordion earlier and who was now acting as night porter. Sara looked in her handbag for aspirin.

"Fahmi doesn't seem to be here," Sam said, and moved

closer. His breath was hot on her right ear, and she moved away. "You smell nice," he said, and came closer again. "Have a drink. One for the wooden road."

"No, really. I've had enough for one evening; in fact, far too much. I'm not used to such quantities of red wine. Is James coming back?" she asked Sara.

"Yes. He went to his room for a book he said he'd promised to lend you if he could remember where he had packed it. He said to wait as he might be some time away and he's ordered coffee for two in half an hour." She yawned. "We're bushed, and we aren't interested in churches like you two are, so we'll go on up."

Jane glanced at Sam apprehensively, hating to be alone with him and deciding that he was very drunk. She looked towards the stairs, willing James to appear, then hung her jacket on the back of a chair and left the guidebook in a prominent position on the table near the door. I needn't wait, and if I go now, she reasoned, James will see the book and take it and I can collect my jacket in the morning. Oh, why didn't he come or why didn't Sam go away and leave her alone?

"Have some orange juice," Sam suggested in a normal, friendly voice. "You can have coffee when Fahmi comes back but some orange will make sure you have no hangover tomorrow. Vitamin C," he added.

"Thank you." She looked at him, surprised that he could show such consideration.

"I'll have to be barman and they can charge it up to me

tomorrow," he said. He went to the bar and came back with two glasses of fresh juice, ice cubes clinking as he walked and swished the orange in the glasses.

"This *is* orange juice?" she asked, with an attempt at humour.

"What the hell?" His face darkened.

"I mean, only that once at a party someone put vodka in my drink, and vodka doesn't taste, does it?"

He sipped his drink and his eyes were calculating. "No vodka in that, baby, I promise you."

Jane drank about a third of the glass of juice and sighed. "That's so much better. I wish I'd stuck to soft drinks tonight. I didn't know that wine would make me so thirsty."

"Drink it up," he said, but she shook her head.

"It's very nice but a bit sweet. I'll drink water when I get to my room or have coffee when James comes down." She smiled. Sam didn't seem so bad now. The orange had gone over her tongue like nectar and she wondered why she had thought it too sweet. It had been delicious, and everything now seemed brighter and better, even the chairs were more elegant than she remembered. The carpet had exotic patterns that she had not noticed and it was wonderful what they had done to the lighting.

She stared at the plain glass globe above her and thought that the dead flies inside it made an exciting pattern. Such colours and such light were enough to make her cry. "It's all so beautiful, Sam," she whispered. She laughed, throwing back her head to show the long line of her throat and pulled her hair back from her face. She had never known her hair feel so smooth and so luxuriant.

"That's right, baby, it's beautiful." His face seemed to fill the room and her head almost exploded with the thought that she was beautiful and desirable and free. She ran out of the door into the warm night. The stars were huge and and she knew that if she climbed the dunes she would be able to touch them.

"Christ, she's having a bad trip," Sam murmured. "Hell, what do I do now? Please come down fast, Jane!" I didn't give her much and she didn't drink it all, he recalled.

He followed her as fast as he could. Now she was singing. "Quiet," he called. "You'll wake everybody."

"Must be quiet," she whispered. "Bye, Sam. I'm going to swim up through that silver lane and sit on the moon." It was too hot for restricting clothes and James had said that girls like her went on the beach with no clothes at all, so she pulled off her blouse and carefully placed it on the ground, then tried to unzip her skirt. Her arms in the moonlight caught the soft pallor of the night and she finally stood in her bikini briefs, high up on a sand dune. Her shoes had joined the trail of discarded clothes and Sam was aghast at what he had done, but roused and excited. He wanted her to come to him willingly; then there would be no hassle.

"I'm happy! I'm happy," she called and the sound reverberated over the dunes.

Sam looked back at the silent hotel, half expecting lights to go on in the windows. It must be her first trip and he wished she'd come down fast. He unzipped his jeans, feeling faintly ridiculous as he had to follow her while holding his pants up as she went from dune to dune like quicksilver. "Come here," he said, but she danced away.

"Say I'm the best dancer in the world, Sam," she ordered.

"Christ almighty, you are!" So white and pure, so unspoiled, with pink-tipped breasts and a pearly body and her hair now in damp swathes clinging to her throat; his for the taking. He was acutely aware of his erection but they were too close to the hotel. He must get her out of this damned moonlight, but she danced away and then faltered.

"Sam?" It was a little girl voice. The night was darker and she heard a voice calling her name from among the poplars. Jane saw the lights fade from the stars and her sweat was cold. She put her arms across her chest and looked up, frightened, as if the wrath of the gods would kill her. Sam was strange, too. She had never seen a naked man except in statues, but Sam wasn't an ancient statue. This man could hurt her. He wasn't the nice Sam who had given her fresh orange juice. She began to weep as she felt the weight of a nameless guilt and sobbed as she walked towards the moon path on the sea to gain redemption.

Sam tried to stop her but she was like a slippery eel. He struggled into his trousers, giving up hope of sex and knowing he must not let her drown. "Jane," he shouted, forgetting the hotel. "Jane, you silly cow, it's Sam! Come here. I won't hurt you."

Two voices were calling her but she went on, to wash away her sins. The sand became soggy underfoot and small fry wriggled away from her toes. Behind her the hotel woke up and put on lights and two voices called her again and again, but she began to cry with deep shuddering sobs and didn't hear them. Her toes, bleeding after being cut on the sharp grass, were hurting badly and she had a cramp in her legs. Her body convulsed in searing spasms and she sank onto the wet sand, instinctively turning her face away from the water.

Strong, ungentle hands seized her and plucked her from the water and she drooped against a cotton shirt smelling of good cologne and cleanliness. She buried her face in it and heard again the voice that had called over the sand. "Jane, my darling, are you all right?" James Fahmi held the naked girl in his arms and an unfamiliar surge of protective rage made him peer back into the darkness where Sam was struggling with a broken zip. James had feared the worst since he found the book and the jacket, and the porter had said that the blonde girl had gone out into the garden with the American and didn't look well.

He had looked for her in the garden and finally on the beach, where he heard her laughing and wondered if he was too late. He found a shoe there, a skirt here and a blouse, weaving a path from side to side on the dunes, and he hated to think what had happened during the time he had taken to find the book he wanted and go down to join her for coffee. He slipped out of his shirt and put it round her, buttoning her arms inside as if in a straitjacket, before lifting her up again and walking back over the dunes.

"Look," Sam said. "It was all a gas. I didn't *do* anything to her."

"If I find that you have, I shall kill you," James said softly, brushing past him and striding back, wondering at her small bones and fragility. His stomach churned when he recalled Sam standing there with his pants in his hands. He had never felt like this about any woman. Who was she, this small, pale girl with the terrible hair who made him want to weep over her?'

The night porter was only mildly curious as he opened the elevator doors for them, and shrugged acquiescence when James ordered coffee in Jane's room, having no wish to stir the wrath he saw in the taut brown face. Soon, he tapped on the door of the room where the blonde girl lay and put the tray on the table. "Cognac?" he asked, but James shook his head and thanked him. "*Nuit*, monsieur."

Jane groaned. She was still wet and James was rubbing her with a rough towel, warming her and stimulating her reactions. He found a sweater in a drawer and slipped it over her head, pulling the soaking hair through in long strands. He twisted the hair in a clumsy knot of towelling and made her sip coffee.

"Too strong," she said and tried to turn her head away, slipping away from his grasp. He sat her on the floor with her back to the chest of drawers and held her firmly pressed against the wood while he held the cup to her lips.

"No," she grumbled. "Orange juice. I want some more orange juice with lots of ice." Her teeth were chattering and she was cold. "Not sweet enough."

James added three lumps of sugar with one hand while his other hand held her firmly, and tried again. She sipped and her head fell forward, her cheek touching his hand. Such a cold, smooth cheek that dipped down to the gentle mouth. He gritted his teeth. "Drink!" he ordered and she finished the cup. He dragged the bedcover from the bed, suddenly too weak to lift her, as if he had walked across the Sahara with her instead of the short distance from the dunes to the hotel.

He sat beside her on the floor and her head was drowsy on his shoulder. He breathed deeply and glanced at the top of her damp head. She was quiet now and would soon be asleep, but he had to know. "Jane?" He shook her gently. She grunted but her eyes wouldn't focus. "Jane? What happened?"

"What happened? I danced. I'm very, very good, James. Did you see me?" He smiled. She knew who he was and trusted him enough to snuggle close. This wasn't a reaction to rape, even when a woman might be willing during an LSD trip. She smelled of the sea and youth and faintly of woman but nothing to suggest that anything had occurred other than a hallucinogenic trip from which she was returning. "I've such a headache, James."

"You'll have a worse one in the morning," he said sternly. "Tell me what happened, Jane. Did anyone hurt you?"

"I had some orange but it was too sweet and I left most of it. Sam gave it to me and was very kind. I went out for some air, I think, and it was beautiful. I never knew it was different in France at night. Sam came with me onto the beach." She wrinkled her nose, trying to remember, and looked down at her bare toes. "Where are my shoes?"

"You left them on the beach." He looked at the bleeding toes encrusted with sand and blood. "Can you sit up on your own now? I have to get some water and antiseptic for those cuts. Would you be more comfortable on the bed?

"No, I'll stay here. I'm quite all right, thank you," she said primly, obviously shocked at the idea that he might see her in bed.

He smiled faintly. All she needs is a ribbon in her hair and an orthodontic brace on her teeth, he thought, and shrugged as if he was caught in an inevitable trap of his own making. "I'll be gone for two or three minutes, Jane. Don't try to move while I'm away," he said. She closed her eyes and nodded, and he hurried back to his own room along the corridor and found Sam slumped against the wall, watching Jane's door. "Get lost!" he said, grimly. "You've done enough for one night."

"I did nothing." Some of the old bravura had returned. "You took your time in there. Good, was she?" Sam sat straighter. "Now she's got the idea, I might make out better tomorrow." He saw the furious expression on the face of the other man and grinned. "Some guys have all the luck. I did the groundwork and in walks James Fahmi and takes the cherry."

James Fahmi stood over him, his fists clenched. "It's times like this that I'm glad I'm not the complete gentleman," he said.

"Hey, *no*! You wouldn't!" Sam tried to struggle up but a well aimed kick caught him under the ribs as he turned. "Christ," he moaned, his left kidney on fire.

"Just one more word about Jane and you'll wish you'd never been born," James said calmly.

"What the hell has it to do with you? She's just some

broad you met on holiday and I've as much right to her as anyone."

"Make the locals if you must but never speak to Jane again except to apologise for a bad joke that went wrong. I'll be charitable and make her believe that you only intended to send her on a trip and stand by to see the fun." His eyes were cold and Sam moved along the wall out of range of the suede boot heavy with sand and sea water.

"I still don't get it. The Sir Galahad bit."

"I haven't time to argue. I have to get some dressings for her feet. They are badly cut." He went to the door of his room, then turned sharply when he heard Sam move. 'Keep away from her, Bradfield. I have other ideas for her." He fetched his first aid box and a packet of tissues and walked back past the speechless man, ignoring him completely.

The door closed and James saw that Jane was nearly asleep. He carried her to the bed and put her face downwards, with her feet over the end of the bed above a bowl of warm water. She sighed as he washed away the sand but seemed to take his ministrations for granted, and hardly winced as the sharp antiseptic stung the cuts. He turned her on her back and covered her feet with a clean towel under the coverlet then drew the duvet up to cover her chest. His hand brushed against the softness and lingered. She smiled at him through half-open eyelids as if he was dear and familiar and the temptation was almost unbearable.

"Thank you, James. My feet don't hurt so much now. Did you find my book?" she asked, as if that was the last thing they had discussed.

"Yes, I found it and shall read it in bed, and tomorrow I'll know as much as you do." He smiled and took her hand. "You must go to sleep. Tomorrow we have a lot to do."

"If my feet hurt, I think I may stay in bed. I still feel a bit hazy and unreal." She looked at him with clear eyes. "What happened to me? Was it something I ate? I didn't really have a tummy upset, but it was very odd."

"Bradfield slipped something into your drink and you were a bit high."

"Was I? Yes, I suppose I was. I've never felt like it before. Everything suddenly seemed brighter and bigger and I felt like taking all my . . ." She blushed. "I must have dreamed it. I could never do anything like that in front of a man."

"Couldn't you, Jane?" His eyes were gentle. "Could you for me?"

She clutched the duvet firmly as if he might whisk it away from her. "I don't do things like that." She looked down, unable to meet his gaze. "I just don't have the figure for it," she said, trying to laugh.

"Ah, but you have. Indeed you have." He patted her hand. "Enough of that for now. Tonight you are quite safe and, I think, a virgin still." She sensed that it was an important question for him and one she had to answer. She blushed and nodded. "That rare and essential virtue," he murmured and kissed her cheek.

"They say that it doesn't matter any more," she began.

"Never believe that," he said. "Tomorrow we shall go to the

Abbaye again if you can walk a little. That is, after you've had your hair cut."

"My hair? I've always worn it long."

"Obviously," he said dryly. "But there have to be changes."

"I don't see what it has to do with you," she said. Her feet felt warmer. She wriggled them under the duvet and decided that they were not hurting nearly as much. "After next week you will go away and you won't have to look at my hair," she said.

"And you will go back to that exciting life, working in the library and having very little hope of taking your degree?"

She bit her lip and tears threatened. "I can try," she said slowly. "I've saved up to buy time and next year I might manage it."

"Wouldn't you rather travel?" She gave him a sweet, uncomprehending smile, as if he had described a pipe dream. "I have to go to Cairo for a while," he said. "I want to take you there – but not if your hair looks like it does now," he added firmly.

"I can't go to Cairo with you!"

"Why not?" He frowned. "Then how am I to show you to my family?"

"Family?"

"Yes, my mother and father and sisters. They will expect to see you before we get married or they will be very offended and might never forgive me."

"*You* are getting married and you want me to be there?"

"*We* are going to be married, my dear child."

"Who said anything about that?" She clutched the duvet again.

"I did." He kissed her again but this time on the mouth. "I didn't want to marry you, Jane, and it made me very angry when I found how much I wanted you, but now, I need you with me forever." He laughed softly. "You *do* love me, Jane. You will want to marry me and do everything in the correct manner, but if you make me wait for too long I shall be under a great strain."

"Do you really love me, James? Not just for . . . that?"

"Silly girl. Go to sleep. Of course I love you."

Chapter Seven

"Damn Adrian," said Robert Blackberne. A small Citroën flashed by towards Deauville, forcing him onto the uneven verge, and the distant whine of motorscooters showed that even here in the quiet of rural Normandy there was nightlife. He kicked an empty can along the road and wondered why he had bothered to leave England when he had a stack of work waiting to be finished in his studio.

The smell of wine and Gaulloise mingled with cooking smells partly reassured him. This was France, the country he loved and had visited so often over the past years whenever he needed to be alone or to work out something in his mind that didn't jell in the academic atmosphere in which he lived, and especially now after the marital pretence that prevailed with Judith.

He pushed open the door to the auberge and stood just inside, watching the men playing cards and a family plowing their way through several courses of food, managing to talk and eat at the same time with amazing facility. He ordered pernod and sat at a table by the window. To meet Antonia again was a shock and he was still reeling from the impact. Surely after all this time, it was nothing more than the revival of a juvenile dream, to feel moved by a woman who had once been dear to him?

He ordered another pernod and sat staring at the room and the people in it without seeing anything but her face in the blue haze of smoke. First it was the face of the immature Antonia, the day she left for Greece with the other girls. Such shy tenderness, such promise in the dark eyes, that it was a superhuman effort to let her go and to take up his parents' offer of time in America, the reward for work well done, when all he wanted was her, to take her and make love to her and keep her forever.

He drained his glass as the image changed to the Antonia he had seen on the beach, talking to her students with authority and humour, a grown-up Antonia with traces of sorrow in her face when she wasn't smiling, and the guarded expression when they had met in the bar, and she had kept her distance, not even shaking his hand as former friends might do. "Bitch," he said softly. She had traded his love for a soft option with Marcel, so why bother to remember her as she had been?

Outside, some men playing boule in the dusty garden asked him to play. It was soothing and mindless and the men took it for granted that being British he had little French to offer, so they smiled and grunted, and laughed when his heavy metal ball won a throw. The stars shone as they had once shone over the poplars at home. Why think of them now? Was it guilt, knowing that he had sent that picture to Adrian as if it meant nothing and was the end of an era and they were finished? He recalled the pain of parting with it, as intolerable as the pain of keeping it where he could see it and remember. Had he really been so mad with rage and jealousy that he could have done that?

"Damn Adrian," he murmured again and missed a pitch so badly that the other men laughed in delighted derision. If we had been lovers, he thought, it might have been different. Antonia would have been faithful to me instead of needing to find outlets for her newly aroused sexuality. An amused murmur greeted yet another clumsy pitch and he grinned his apologies. Adrian must have known that Antonia was taking this course before he telephoned, offering accommodation at the hotel with the quiet company of the professor and all the facilities he needed for painting and relaxation.

Another pernod was thrust into his hand and Robert was aware of emptiness and the beginnings of a lightheaded warning. He ordered soup and bread and felt better when he was full of good, simple, country padding. The card school was getting noisy and a third carafe was on the table, so Robert walked out, breathing the mingled scents of broom and salt, and diesel from the huge *camions* that made him once again seek the shelter of the bank.

He wondered if he could face meals at the hotel. At first he had been frozen and felt a kind of dumb acceptance that he would see Antonia across the dining room each day, but now he knew he couldn't bear it. He saw her face again as it had been today, polite, too bright, with carefully cut hair and an

119

air that said she was used to looking very good in expensive clothes. His face hardened. Her husband was far away, she bore every sign of a prosperous lifestyle, but she wore a cheap Greek skirt. Had that holiday in France and Italy, culminating in the Greek Islands, left her with a residual desire for her Greek lovers? Was the skirt a giveaway to her secret yearnings for some crude virile Greek who had stolen her heart as well as her body?

Lights shone from every window in the hotel as he approached and he could hear laughter. A girl ran from the house, pursued by two men and followed by others, girls and boys from the village on their way to the beach. A light flared as someone lit a beach fire, using far too much petrol, and he saw the big American lugging a crate of drinks along the yielding sandy path. I'm getting old, Robert decided. Once, that would have been Robert Blackberne, making more noise then any of them, drinking, singing and chasing the girls.

But Antonia would never sleep with him. He stood on the edge of the dunes and looked up at the stars. She was scared of casual sex and he had done nothing to reassure her, thinking only of the urge and the satisfaction and not of the tenderness she needed, until the night before she left for Greece and they had come very near to the act of love. She had tears in her eyes as she turned away and he suddenly knew that he must have her, not for the night or a passing lust, but because she was Antonia, sweet and beautiful and tender, who loved him in spite of his clumsy brashness and who wanted to marry him.

He stared into the night with cold, desperate eyes. What had happened to change her? How could a girl like that have acted as she did as soon as she got to Greece and they were free to sleep on beaches with the moon goddess bending her cynical rays on sleeping lovers? He listened to the beach noises, the laughter and the sea. She must have changed completely. She must have been as the letters and photographs indicated, or tonight the scars long healed would bleed and gape again if she had feelings.

Adrian had never believed the letters and had tried to find out who had sent them anonymously. They must have come from one of her party; the postmarks were from that area and changed as they moved to other campsites.

"I was a blind, mad fool," he said. "I never asked Antonia if it was true." He shut his eyes but couldn't shut out the truth. He had taken the word of a malicious stranger and buried his bitterness in the soft and willing bosom of the woman he had married, using his anger to put the gold ring on her finger, the marriage sealed before he woke from the stupor of shattered pride and realised that he had acted too hastily. Judith knew it was a mistake but had clung to the man she had wanted ever since she went to university, even when his response grew cold and he refused her pleas for a proper marriage, with a family and herself at home, wallowing in domesticity.

The sighing of high branches led him back beyond the hotel to a path upturning to a small hill. It reminded him of the avenue at the side of the campus, with waving poplars making the curiously individual moan of tall trees. Here it was quiet, with the road and the beach hidden from sight and sound and nothing but the stars and the trees above him. He took off his zipped cotton jacket and lay on the grass with it under his head. Something moved in the bushes, but nothing that disturbed his sombre thoughts. The moon was high in a warm black mantle, the sea remote and impersonal and the hotel contained only people with no interest in Robert Blackberne.

There was nobody to advise him; he was alone as he had rarely been alone, even when Judith was picking a fight and work had gone stale. This was isolation from human warmth and love and friendship, and he was the only one who could choose what the future must hold.

He gazed up at the Milky Way, knowing that his marriage was at an end – if it had ever really started. Now he must go back and make the break final, instead of finding more and more excuses for being away from the apartment and Judith.

Antonia was more beautiful now that the quirks of adolescence had been ironed out, and her naive eyes had become steady and sad. Robert took little satisfaction in thinking that the sadness meant an unsatisfactory marriage. If she was trapped and couldn't have lovers then she would be miserable. "Hell!" he said. "It doesn't make sense." Seeing her again and knowing the Antonia that was, he couldn't believe that she was some kind of nymphomaniac. He took a deep breath and knew he must get away, never see her again. New Zealand had been good and he'd sold work there. There was every chance of a permit to stay if he went as a visitor and applied to work there as a resident soon after, once he was free. I need never come back, he decided, but the idea gave him no joy. He reached for the piece of wood that had been sticking into his back for the past five minutes and threw it clear of the place where he lay. It hit a tree, scattering pieces of rotten bark.

"Oh!" It was a woman's voice and Robert leaped to his feet and made for the sound, sensing her pain. "Oh, it went in my eye," she said.

"I'm terribly sorry. I had no idea that anyone was here," he said, bending over the trembling figure. He handed her a handkerchief. "Did it go right in?"

"Just a fragment of loose bark, I think." She dabbed her eye, blinking, tears running down her cheeks. She swayed and he put a hand on her shoulder and Antonia saw that it was Robert Blackberne. She tried to laugh. "I know you didn't want to see me again, but must you throw sticks at me?" She wiped her eyes and handed the handkerchief back to him. It smelled of tobacco and turps and she wondered if it had introduced more foreign bodies than it removed, so she found a piece of clean tissue in her own pocket and wiped her eyes again. "I'm fine now," she asserted.

"Are you sure?" He stood awkwardly, unable to see her face clearly as she stood with her back to the moonlight. He stuffed his handkerchief back in his pocket. "Can I get you a drink?"

"No, thank you." It neither gave him encouragement nor yet said goodbye and he relaxed slightly and squinted up at the trees. "Are you enjoying the course?"

Her own tension slackened. "It's quite fun. The students are the usual mix but I enjoy it. Not a lot of talent except for James

Fahmi and one of the women, but if they can lose themselves in doing what they enjoy for even two weeks, then why worry about exhibitions?"

"The Egyptian?"

"He's half English," she said. "I feel rather sorry for him. He doesn't know quite what he's doing here and what to do next. He has talent and could paint seriously but his main interest is history. His family business prevents him from doing either for long, but he's the type to use what spare time he has to the best advantage, perhaps making more progress with everything he attempts than someone with all the time in the world to follow one fulltime interest."

"Is he married?"

She looked up, sharply. "No, he says he hasn't met the right woman yet." She smiled. "He should marry to please his family, and if they left him alone to choose, he might do so, but when there is coercion it makes even the most suitable woman who might be paraded for his benefit by a loving parent seem less than attractive."

"You seem to know a lot about him."

"Not really, but I have learned about people." Her voice seemed to come from far away, although if he reached out he could have touched her.

The wisp of cloud left the moon. "You look very well," he said.

"And you, Robert. The beard suits you."

"You said I should grow one; do you remember?"

"No," she lied. "I expect it was Judith."

"She hates it. She hates most of what I do." He looked down at the darkly shining hair and wanted to touch it.

"I'm sorry," she said. "I hoped you were happy." She glanced up and saw the misery in his eyes. "You must have been very much in love with her at first, to have married so suddenly." The hard edge was deliberate; she wanted to wound, to drag out his old emotions and to revenge herself on the painful years.

"*No!*"

"Then why? Wasn't it stupid to get married so quickly?"

"I had to get you out of my mind."

"Why? I was coming back to university, not staying forever in Greece, sleeping rough with every Stavros and Iannis who wanted me," she said quietly. Her hands were like cold lead and her heart overflowed with anguish.

"Don't," he whispered.

"Why not? That's what you believed, wasn't it?" She walked more quickly. "Why did you come here, Robert? After all this time, why couldn't you just leave me alone instead of disrupting my time here?"

"I didn't know you were here, Antonia. Adrian suggested that I came to work here while the Prof was teaching." She looked at him with complete disbelief. "I'm telling you the truth. He must have known that you wouldn't want me here, so I can't think why he did it. Devious he might be, but Adrian is never deliberately cruel unless he sees a reason for it, like stirring students to action."

"Well, you're here now and you have all the facilities you

need. There's even a model ready and waiting if you don't mind painting little French tarts."

"Jacqueline?"

"Yes, but I'd be grateful if you wouldn't, as Sam seems to have the same idea and with him things might get out of hand."

"Do you think she's a tart?"

"Not really. I think she's a simple country girl who might easily have her head turned by people like Sam. I suspect that she's a virgin who would scream blue murder and rape if anyone got down to real business. She may look easy, but people are not always as they seem," she said. "It's dangerous to take what appears to be the truth to be just that unless you are sure," she added quietly.

"You wear a Greek skirt. A souvenir of a wonderful holiday?"

"I bought it last year when Marcel took me there on business. It was an impulse buy and I find it very cool and comfortable to wear it here. Marcel hates it," she said.

"The skirt? Or because he knows that you have a special feeling for the country?" The casual mockery didn't come off and he sounded bitter and condemning.

"I love Greece," she said, "as I love France and Italy, each in its own way, but I don't love the entire Greek nation nor have I been made love to by any of those very attractive men."

"I thought," he began, and hurried after her, further into the avenue. "I was told that you had rather a . . . good time when you went backpacking."

She turned to face him and the moonlight shone on her tense, suddenly thin face. "And you believed it!"

"Antonia." His hands fell to his sides and she saw that he was crying. It was the moment of triumph of which she had dreamed, to have him before her, unhappy and ashamed, out of love with Judith and knowing how much she despised him. She savoured it for a full minute, but shared his suffering. "Can you ever forgive me?" he asked at last.

"No, I think not," she said. "I can forgive you for coming here and even enjoy your company if you wish, but how can I forgive the years that have gone, been taken from me and wasted?" Her cry was low and agonised and scalding tears began, slowly at first, running unheeded down her face and onto her thin blouse.

"But you married Marcel," he remembered. "I imagined that you were blissfully happy, living in luxury."

"Happy?" Her voice was husky and the words came painfully. "Marcel wrote those letters and sent the photographs that he insisted were just for fun and to give the locals a thrill to be snapped with a pretty girl. He waited for a whole year after we were married, then he told me, and enjoyed every word. Until then I had no idea why you dropped me so cruelly. Didn't you ever wonder about him? He was with us for most of the time in a group with geology students. He read my diary and found out about you." She sniffed audibly. "I'm too tidy. I had lists of addresses in the back and references to you and he soon caught on that you were my serious boyfriend."

"But you do love him?"

"I hate him. I *hate Marcel* and I *hate men!*" Her sobs died into cold despair as she tried to go back to the hotel. Robert took her arm roughly and pulled her towards him. His mouth was hard and desperate on hers and she knew that she was drowning in their tears, in the empty space that should have been filled with love, and the angry knowledge that they had been cheated. His dear, familiar arms were as she remembered but his lips were more practiced, and his body was as young and hard as ever.

She clung to him and they sank into the shadows of the poplars. He gazed into her face. "I never stopped loving you," he told her.

"Oh, Robert! Why can't we put the clock back?"

"We have the future," he insisted and kissed her again. She leaned against him and he caressed the bare spot between skirt and blouse. He kissed her hair and closed his eyes as she put a hand up to his cheek, rediscovering the contours of his face. "Judith and I are finished," he said, and she felt his whole body tense as he waited for her reaction, dreading what she might say.

"Marcel won't be easy," she whispered, and shuddered as she recalled the cold eyes of the man she had married. "He's very possessive; at times I'm afraid of him, and yet when he first told me he loved me and wanted to protect me, it seemed a haven."

"Don't go back."

She gasped. "I must. I have to go back."

"Why?" He kissed her again and she stroked his beard,

wondering at his beauty, the smell of him and the growing sensation that they had never been apart.

"We both have to go back," she said firmly. "You must go home, if only to see that Judith is all right. I have to get some things sorted out, too."

"Promise me that you will come to me?"

"I never went away," she said softly. A breeze came in from the sea and the trees whispered of love. Robert lowered her onto his jacket and buried his face in her breasts. Her thighs softened with desire and she caught his hand to press on the silky mound palpable through her thin skirt. His mouth was gentle but demanding and the trees gave them shelter as the pulse of love quickened and joined them in a mad climax of a new union that seemed unending, fierce and tender, promising them joy for ever.

"If only," she said as the storm subsided, but he stifled her words with more kisses, enfolding her gently and making her almost die of tenderness.

"No ifs, my darling. We go on from here together."

They talked of everything and nothing, and the past was more real than the time they had spent with other partners. Even Marcel was unreal and light years away now. They made love again more leisurely and with growing pleasure in each other, touching and kissing and finding the delight of just lying close together, in love. For the first time, Antonia knew the heaven of after-love, the joy of loving and giving and knowing that the wonderful glow could last. The final barriers in her mind dissolved into hope, and she was warm and contented.

The beach party was still singing as Robert led her back to the hotel. He left her at the door of her room and kissed the tip of her nose. "Be a good example to your class," he told her. "And wipe that stupid smile away before they see you."

"Speak for yourself. You look far too happy for a serious artist with work on his mind." She closed the door and went to the shower. The water washed away the dust of the grove, the gentle spray soothing the soreness of their first savage lovemaking, and her erect nipples relaxed into fulfilled softness. With heavy limbs, she climbed on to the bed and reclined on the top of the bedclothes, smiling.

There was a small calendar in the back of her diary and she made a cross on the date when she had met Robert again, just as she had made marks to note happenings at school that had seemed important at the time, and later, exam dates and times to be noted when she had end-of-term happenings at university. It was satisfying to see the small cross and Robert's initial once more where she could look at it and know that on that moonlit night, they had become real lovers for the first time.

They would have several days together, time enough to discuss the future. She put her hands behind her head and watched the changing lights and shadows on the ceiling as the moon filtered through and brightness from the lamps in the garden made dancing shadows when the breeze stirred the trees. Marcel receded further and further away and Robert gave her confidence. The fact that they had made love also gave her strength. Marcel could never take that away now.

She smiled, forcing herself to think of him rationally. He

would be furious when he discovered that she wasn't pregnant and she had to cling to the memory of Robert's face to stop the shiver that made her pull up a sheet to cover her naked body. Marcel was a puzzle she hoped she would never have to solve in the future. He had pursued her to possess her and had admitted that he wanted a child to be dark like him, had known that with Antonia for a mother his children would fit his scheme of what he wanted in his offspring.

He had never seemed to want children until now, she recalled, but somewhere in his mind he must have had the idea that he must marry a dark-haired woman, necessary for a perfect reproduction of himself. She remembered his real preference was for Junoesque blondes and she had once asked him in anger and pain, after a particularly nauseating night of sex when he had bought yet another picture of a fair-haired nude of Rubens-type proportions, why he didn't take a blonde mistress who might enjoy his kind of sex, instead of using pictures of them to turn him on to make savage love to his wife.

Antonia thought back to the party with which Marcel was travelling now; to the geologists and co-ordinators of the group and she remembered that Gerda Blaum would be there. She smiled. Gerda looked as if she had stepped out of one of Marcel's pictures and Antonia enjoyed using the phrase that Sam had voiced when he thought that Jackie fancied him. Gerda really did have the hots for Marcel and in primitive conditions, with no other outlet for sex, it wouldn't be surprising if he succumbed to her earthy charms.

131

Antonia sighed. Gerda couldn't produce the right kind of child for Marcel, but she could be a possible second wife if he had the child he wanted. The first of the beach party were coming back and motorscooters revved up to take the boys back to the village. It's no use, Antonia decided. I shall ask for a divorce and, as we are not having a baby, maybe he'll cut his losses if Gerda has her way.

She put out the light; not that she was tired, but she wanted to show no light under the door in case some enthusiast came to tell her about the party. Her eyes grew large in the darkness when she remembered that she was no longer taking contraceptives. "I could get pregnant," she said. "But this one would be Robert's."

Chapter Eight

"'*Stay me with flagons, comfort me with apples, for I am sick with love.*'"

Antonia laughed. "I can't stay. I have a lecture to give in five minutes and I can't appear in front of a class with calvados coming out of my ears. It's time you did some work, too." She laughed. "But I must admit that in that awful shirt and those trunks, you do look rather like a sexy Bacchant." She dodged his grasping hand. "A bit hairy, but so are most of the famous artists, and I adore the beard." She poured the rest of the liqueur onto the grass under the poplars. "A libation to the gods," she said. "Send us lasting happiness."

Robert kissed her hand and she hurried away, her eyes wet. Why did I say that? Was their newly awakened love so fragile that it needed prayers to pagan gods to give it substance? She glanced at her watch and hurried to her room to collect her clipboard and notes. The eyes that reflected as she tidied her hair were luminous and she dabbed her temples with cologne to calm her pulse, but as she approached the group by the geraniums, she was unobserved. The students had already started painting, aware that time was running out for them. Two more days and they would leave her to clear up and pack their bags before making a leisurely return to England, unless she decided to go back with them.

Strange, she thought. It's unlikely that we shall ever meet again unless they enrol in some future class that I might take. For them there would be other classes, other venues, and some had certainly benefited from this two weeks. She concentrated on the work of one woman who had shown a great deal of improvement and dedication and who would go home spurred on to bigger things. She looked up and smiled gratefully as Antonia suggested improvements. "Will you be taking any more classes like this, Antonia?" she asked.

The others paused to hear her reply. "Surely you've all had enough of my bossy approach," she said lightly.

"Don't be daft. We've learned an awful lot with you," Sara said, eyeing her latest effort with affection. "They'll never believe I did this," she said with satisfaction. "I shall hang it on the wall in the living room and everyone will have to look at it. Trouble is, I shall have to get different loose covers for the suite as geraniums just won't match."

"It's very good," Antonia said. "You've all done something worth keeping and I hope it makes you go on and meet other artists and sit in on other classes. There's nothing like talking to like-minded people about your work and using them as sounding-boards. Talking shop can be fascinating."

"But are you doing this again?"

"Yes. I've decided that I enjoy it and I shall write to the organisers to accept several other jobs they have offered me." There was a buzz of speculation as to where these would be, but she said she didn't know exact dates and places so they must ask for the next schedule as soon as it was printed if they wanted to have a choice of venue. "There will be other tutors who can offer you more than I can, if for instance you want to do watercolours or pastels or etchings, and they might be good for you," she added. She hesitated. "I can't give you my home address as I'm not sure where I shall be living after next month, but you have the address of the organiser and if you lose that, then write to Robert at the university and he'll help you. He told me last night that he has accepted a lecturer's post there and will live on campus in a small cottage." He had also hinted that the post of senior lecturer would fall vacant in two years time and was his for the asking.

She moved along to the next easel, then sat on the wall until someone asked for help. Adrian was a devil! He had planned it all. She could think of him now without resentment. Did he realise that his interference might spark off this devouring flame? Did he know that he might have destroyed her marriage and the whole comfortable background of her life with Marcel?

She shivered. That was another life; it held nothing of Normandy sunshine, bright flowers, gentle evenings and easy ways. It had none of Robert's all-pervading and tender love, none of his offhand caring, more real than the conventional public solicitousness that Marcel showed to the world.

Everyone seemed absorbed and she had time to go into Caen

while they were working. There were items to be picked up, like processed film and more turps substitute and she wanted to be alone for a while, to think objectively. She heard Robert call as she climbed into the buggy and waved as if in answer to his goodbye. This was her last chance to be quite alone before she had to do paperwork and organise the last day with her students. Luggage and passports had to be got ready and canvases packed and she knew that at least one student would need some more currency to get him past duty free.

She made for the castle and stood high above the town, hardly seeing the skilful reconstruction of the old city. Marcel was due back from South America in a few weeks and she just wasn't ready to face him. She walked down to the post office, not expecting any mail but recalling that she had given her housekeeper the poste restante address in case of any word from Marcel. After a short delay, she was handed two letters and she felt a physical shock as she saw Marcel's handwriting.

The café on the corner was noisy and the dry diesel-filled air blew scraps of paper under the metal and plastic chairs. Antonia ordered coffee and left it to go cold. She held the unopened letter and wished that Robert was with her to give her strength. A siren whined in the distance and traffic was building up with the afternoon commuters and the coming back to life of Caen after the long lunchbreak.

Shoppers went by, unaware of the pale-faced woman with the aching heart hidden beneath the summer tan and bright gypsy clothes. Children sucked the pointed ends of freshly-made folded crêpes and laughed when chocolate dripped down the edges. One child was light-haired among the sturdy dark-tressed little French children who strutted like bright starlings, chattering and pushing. Marcel's children, she thought, and smiled faintly; but not by my making. Mine will have red hair, she decided. If I have Robert's child it will bear his stamp, making it his as surely as he has made me his after all this time.

She slit the envelope and noticed that it was dated the day after Marcel had arrived in South America. She felt cold but smiled as she read confirmation of what she had already known would happen. The women in the party had been left to do the routine chores in the base camp while the macho males went on to the interesting fieldwork. Antonia knew that one woman had better qualifications than Marcel, but she could well imagine that he had brushed aside such trivia with a laugh and loads and loads of sweet, sweet charm.

"We decided that we needed one woman," he wrote, "so Gerda is coming with us. How are you? I hope to hear good news soon. Please send me reports as soon as you have them and at regular intervals. I shall expect you to attend all classes and clinics suggested and make sure that you have specialist treatment if necessary."

A prize cow after artificial insemination couldn't have better care, she thought. She reached for her handbag. The headache was slight but had started as soon as she saw his writing. She felt clumsy and rather bloated. Panic filled her. Perhaps by some terrible miracle of ovulation she was pregnant and the child would be Marcel's. She tried to recall what the symptoms of pregnancy were, but when she went to the lavatory she discovered that her period had started and her bloated feeling was merely water retention. She breathed again. This made it certain that no child now could be from Marcel. If I become pregnant, it will be Robert's child.

She stuffed the letters into her bag and went back to the buggy. Warm air brushed her hair as she drove slowly back, revelling in the sights and sounds of France that would make her homesick for the winding lanes and the afternoon light for the rest of her life. With Marcel, this would have been just another planned luxury holiday, but as she parked the car and walked under the poplars she smelled the damp earth and was contented.

Jacqui was in reception, dressed more soberly than at any time during the previous two weeks and Charles sat with her, looking serious. "We're all going to miss this place," Antonia said.

"Yeah," he said and chewed gum, trying to look nonchalant.

"You have everything ready for the off?" Antonia asked.

"Yeah, everything ready to go and next week she'll be teasing some other unlucky bugger." Jacqui smiled. "She's all tease and no do," he added.

"Stupid little cunt," Jacqui said with pride.

"You shouldn't teach her things like that. What happens when she trots out that phrase when she meets someone with no sense of humour?"

"Boy, I'd love to see it! It would pay her for all the angst."

He laughed and took Jacqui by the hand. "Come on, I'll teach you some more words." He dragged the giggling girl into the sunshine and they disappeared under the shade. Antonia heard them laughing and smiled. If only life was that simple. She checked to see that she wasn't needed and went to her room, where Robert was sitting by the window. He turned as the door closed behind her.

"Had a good session?" she asked.

"I've done no work. I'd have come with you but you went off like a streak of lightning."

"Sorry," she said. "You did say that you wanted to sketch the nephew of the proprietor, didn't you?"

He snorted. "I asked him to come dressed as he was last week but he arrived in his Sunday suit with his hair slicked back with some unmentionable grease. I couldn't use him so I contemplated my life and my navel under the trees."

"And?" Her eyes searched for reassurance in the sombre face.

"We can't go on like this."

"No? You mean it's a mistake?"

He put a hand under her chin and kissed her softly. "The only mistake I made about you was long ago. This time, it's got to be permanent, with no hangups, forever."

"Judith and Marcel might have other ideas."

"Judith will divorce me. She said as much."

"When was this?"

"I telephoned. I said I had met you again and we want to be married. I also told her that I was accepting the job at the university, which she said she'd hate, so in a way it will be a relief all round. She can keep the apartment and everything in it as far as I'm concerned and I shall have you. Judith has money of her own and will do nicely." His hands slipped under her skirt and pressed her to his body. She kissed him but drew away. "All right; later," he said. "I can't get enough of you, my darling, but for the sake of appearances I suppose we'd better go down to the bar."

"Not later."

"Aren't you on the Pill?"

"I was until just before I came here, but as I didn't think I'd be seduced while Marcel was away I thought I'd give my headaches a rest."

"And you weren't worried?"

"No," she said. "Whatever Marcel does when he finds out about us, I want to have your child." They clung together until voices receded downstairs, reminding them that dinner was nearly ready and the class would be gathering in the bar. "We can now behave with suitable decorum until we go home," she said. "It will give me time to concentrate on my work," she added with mock severity.

Sam sat in a corner, drinking pernod and eyeing two new arrivals from Paris, a mother and daughter awaiting the arrival of Papa at weekends. For now they were alone, planning to take in Deauville and a little culture while he was in his office during the week. Martine looked pensive over her watered wine but her dark eyes glinted when she saw Sam's admiring glance. Her mother watched his face as if discovering something that she had missed and Antonia wondered which he would make, the mother or the daughter.

"What are your plans, Sam?" Antonia asked and the two women tried to understand what she was saying as if it might concern them.

"Might stay on and brush up my French," he said. "I've a bit more time to kill before I go back to the rig and this place suits me." He winked and took another sip of pernod and Antonia laughed. He was so blatant, but very attractive in his own way, and in her heart she wished him luck.

James Fahmi lit a cigarette and ignored Bradfield, taking Jane to a far corner to drink her aperitif. Her hair was light and fluffy, short now and even more blonde under the hot sun, and her skin had a lustre of health and happiness. It was a relief for her to allow James to make all the decisions and she seemed to float on a cloud of bliss.

"I've posted off my resignation," she said, catching her breath at the thought of her own boldness. "James and I are going to write a book about Norman influences in Britain. He wants me to stay at home once we are married." She blushed. "I'm going to meet his family in Cairo. Isn't it wonderful, Antonia?"

"Is that what you really want?" Antonia asked anxiously.

Jane sighed with contentment. "I never thought I could be so happy." She blushed. "You've no idea how sweet and protective he is, and he wants to be married as soon as he can fix it."

"You are very lucky," Antonia said sincerely. It isn't the fact that she is marrying James Fahmi that makes her lucky, she decided, but the fact that she really wants to marry him and is willing to have her whole life organised by him. It's Marcel and me all over again, she realised with a sense of shock. Or rather, it's Marcel and me if I had been a weak and pliant personality and had been really in love with him, content to be his slave and possession.

She looked at the two heads bent over a very new book with fine illustrations. They had work and interests in common, too, which she had never enjoyed with Marcel, so maybe the faults in her marriage were not entirely one-sided. Antonia smiled. Jane and James would share love and work and become completely absorbed in their own little world. Jane was so young and innocent, with the long-legged look of the eternal schoolgirl, the ever-virginal child bride, and when she was fifty, she would still have the slightly ingenuous eyes, with children and books to fill her life. Antonia laughed softly. Lucky man; she might even do all his indexing!

Suddenly she was sad. "I think you need something less depressing than pernod," Robert said, taking away her glass. She glanced up sharply." It hardly shows at all," he said, "but it's there, isn't it? Don't panic now, my darling."

"It's all been quite an experience, just being here," she said simply.

"Not all shock and horror?" His eyes were tender.

"No," she replied, "but you're right. No spirits, and I'll stick to wine and mineral water tonight. I have to think clearly."

"Isn't it simple?" She shook her head, unable to reply as Sara and Glenda paused by the table and smiled. "Yes, come and join us," Robert said. "Antonia has the blues because she loves you all and hates to lose you."

"Now, isn't that nice!" said Sara, and Antonia sent a flicker of gratitude towards her lover. "We'll miss you, too. I can't wait to tell them at home all we've done and show off my snaps. I have a few more in the camera so I must use them up tomorrow before we pack. You've got some too, Glenda, so we have to be up early to take pictures of the hotel." She prattled on, allowing the silent pair to retreat into their own thoughts, protecting them from other attempts at conversation from some of the party who liked answers and contributing views. Clever of Robert to sense that their best chance of privacy was inside a voluble group. Sara doesn't want us to talk, she just wants us to listen or appear to do so.

"This might be the very last time I eat those tiny fish in cream. I asked Madame and she said they are on the menu again tonight. When I get back I want to make lots of little pots of *crème vanille* and I think I'll try croissants," Glenda said as they moved to the dining room. "Aren't you glad I made you come here?"

"I thought it was me who did the bullying," Sara said. "But what does it matter? I feel a different person and you really did need a change." They argued happily and Sara said that she intended having a French evening and inviting the neighbours. "I'll leave it until you come to stay next month," she said.

"Do you really feel better for this fortnight away?" Antonia asked.

"Wonderful! I shall carry on with classes now and go to weekend seminars in England knowing that I can mix with people and not feel awkward," Glenda said. She laughed self-consciously. "It's funny, but when Mother was alive, I hardly saw another soul outside of the family. Looking after her and coping with everything else, and then my husband being ill, I was very much alone. If anyone called in to chat, Mother would find something she wanted me to do and made it so plain that they weren't welcome that sometimes I went to my room and cried afterwards, knowing that they wouldn't come back and I'd lost another couple of friends." She wiped her plate with bread to soak up the sauce and ate the last scrap. "I felt as if I was trapped forever and that after she died I could never fit into life outside again. You think I'm silly, don't you?"

"No," Antonia said firmly. "We all know just how you felt."

Glenda looked surprised. "That's another thing. I thought I was the only one to be like that, but when I started art classes and talked to some of the others who were widowed or divorced, I found we had that in common, and many other things too. We all needed to get out and mix more."

"Yes," Robert said softly. "It's like standing on the edge of a wide, empty circle and not daring to put a foot inside it. The past was bad but it *is* familiar and you know the worst of it and you wonder if the empty space of the future can be filled with something better." He saw the solemn faces and laughed. "It takes the same courage to put a sweep of vivid paint across a virgin canvas." They laughed but Antonia bent over her plate. How did he know of her sudden dread of the future? Could it be better than the one she had endured with Marcel for so long that it had become a habit?

What if the fault is all mine, she wondered. Maybe I can't have a deep and lasting relationship with any man. She glanced up, loving the line of his brow and the slight bitterness that the beard couldn't hide. He had suffered and was still suffering. Could her love wash away his sadness or would she only deepen the lines that she had noticed only today?

Sam had managed to be odd-man-out and paused by the table of the French women, all hesitant and self-deprecating, and when Antonia looked again he was firmly ensconced in the spare seat intended for Papa at weekends.

"Which one will he have?" Robert whispered.

"The mother," Antonia said. "She won't let the daughter have a chance there and the girl is most likely a virgin, while Mother is still attractive and knows her way around." She smiled. "That's if Jacqui doesn't suddenly fancy Sam after Charles leaves."

"That, I'd like to see," Robert said. "It could be worth watching if we stayed a while."

"No, I can't stay. I must go back. There are things to do."

He touched her hand briefly. "We have tomorrow. Don't do your mental packing yet." He poured more wine and glanced at Jane. "Did you find out what really happened on the beach?"

"No, James shut up like a clam and Sam seemed almost

frightened. I think he slipped something into Jane's drink and she had a bad trip. The bar boy said as much, but I didn't enquire too deeply as they seem to have sorted everything out between them with no lasting harm. I don't think Sam will do that again, and it certainly gave James the shock he needed to realise that there was more to Jane than a guide to ancient tombs!"

Robert smiled. "He's welcome to her. I prefer someone with a touch of the wild side."

"Don't say that, Robert. You would never describe me like that if you saw me at home." She tried to see herself as she had been with Marcel, and the thought of her well-appointed house was stifling.

"Home?"

"No, not home. The place where I lived with Marcel," she said. "Home will be anywhere that we are together, here in a hotel that would fill Marcel with amused revulsion, in my room, or in the poplar grove where I lost my soul and my true virginity."

"Don't look at me like that," he said, "or I shall grab you and carry you off."

"What did you say?" asked Sara. "You two are always whispering." She eyed them with ill-concealed curiosity. "Talking about old times?" she enquired dryly.

"No, the new ones are better," said Robert. "We find we have a lot in common."

"I suppose so." Sara was only half convinced that the couple hadn't arranged this time away from their respective partners. She sighed. It was all right for some. They'd go back and pick up the threads again as if nothing had happened. If I had a naughty weekend, Paul would see it in my face, she thought wistfully. "Will you be giving another talk before we leave, Antonia?"

"Yes, I'll be ready at ten tomorrow for a short talk, then we can do any last minute shopping and have a farewell dinner tomorrow evening along the road in that new place." Antonia smiled. "It's on the firm but you can buy your own drinks." The dinner had been Robert's idea. If they all had something new to enjoy, she could just sit and smile and feel detached. She found that she really did want to give them a farewell party. They might not know it but they had all in some way contributed to her new sense of freedom of spirit.

If only she could be confident of a lasting freedom, physically, legally and completely. Robert was sketching again, stroking the small pad briskly with a soft pencil and Sara went to look over his shoulder. "It's you, Antonia, but he's made you look too sad. You can't be *that* sorry to lose us!" She took the pad from him and handed it across to Antonia. It showed a beautiful woman with sad eyes and gently quizzical lips.

He knows how uncertain I am and that I can't believe I can change my situation, she thought. She smiled, willing him to see her courage. "Make me smile," she said. "Draw for your dinner tomorrow and I'll let you have crayfish." She laughed impishly. "It will serve you right if you have to draw me again and again so that the others can have copies of their laughing, carefree tutor."

He drew her again and handed the paper to Sara. "Have it

photocopied if you really want it," he suggested and put away his pad. "I think I'll stay in France and sketch the tourists. If I buy a Breton beret and a striped T-shirt I can pass for a Basque and flog these for fabulous sums. Who will stay with me and chat up the punters?"

"I'd love to," giggled Sara, "but my old man would go spare."

"Well, if you've finished with me, I think I'll go to bed. I have some paperwork to finish and a little more mending." She gave a warning glance to Robert. "I need this time alone to get myself sorted," she said lightly. "Goodnight, everyone." She walked towards the stairs aware that Robert wanted to follow her, but she tried to convince herself that he too needed space. He's never liked being nailed down, she recalled, and he might enjoy talking to the others for a change, as they couldn't make love now.

She thought of Robert Blackberne the artist, and not just her lover. His sketch pad went everywhere with him, ready to record interesting faces and to make notes of colours and textures. She had seen him blind to everything but the canvas on which he worked, ignoring the plaintive whinges of a model and impervious to hunger or cold. This was the artist she remembered. Would her love sap away this white heat of diligence?

For once, she waited for the elevator and felt depressed. When I'm over this week, I shall laugh again and feel civilised, she thought. The lift came and she opened the shaky wrought-iron door. People passed on their way to the garden or Reception and someone ran up the stairs while the lift slowly rose. She came to her landing and walked listlessly into her room.

Tomorrow, France would give her a gentle push and she would have to face the fact that Marcel would not be in South America forever. I'm not ready to return to his house. I have to go back and unlock that door and I can't face it. She pushed open the door of her bedroom and saw that once again the girl had closed the shutters tightly over the window, blocking out all sun and air. She went over and flung them back, letting in the soft breeze. The moon shone over the garden and the tall trees whispered. The path of the moon was distant on the glimpse of water that she could just discern beyond the dunes and the sea was calm.

"If it doesn't work out, I'll kill myself," she said.

Hands on her shoulders made her turn sharply. "Never, never say that again. *Never*, do you hear?"

"Robert," she said weakly. He seemed to have arms that could cradle her whole body. He carried her to the bed and knelt beside her, his face on her breast. "I told you not to come here," she said.

"And leave you here biting your nails up to your elbows with guilt and panic?" He caressed her with gentle fingers and soft kisses, soothing rather than stimulating and observing the age-old taboos. She was touched by his care and restraint and knew just how much he truly loved her. "Have you written to him?" he asked.

"No. I had two letters from the first camp and I expect to

hear nothing until he gets down from the rift valley again. I am supposed to send a detailed account of my health."

"He'll have a shock when he hears you aren't pregnant."

"I have no intention of telling him just yet," she replied.

"Why not? You can stress that this means you have no need to stay together, that you have met me again and we both know the whole truth about him and who we have to thank for one horrible misunderstanding. He hasn't a leg to stand on! He must know that you will come back to me, where you belong."

"You make it sound so easy, but you don't know Marcel."

"Well, you have to make up your mind soon. You have an air ticket and I have a rail and sea passage booked, so say we meet up in seven days time? I think the expression is, your place or mine?"

"No," Antonia sat up and brushed the hair from her face. "We can't."

"Why not?" His eyes were cool. "Face it, darling. There is no going back now. I am your husband and you are my wife and we are in love. There is never going to be a time when we are not together."

"I'm frightened. Give me another week to sort out some things and to decide what I want to tell Marcel and then I'll come and help you get the cottage straight. It is empty, I hope?"

"Another week but no more. The cottage idea is good. You might as well have it just as you want it from the start. It's unfurnished and I can clean it up and do the walls before you come, and we can go to sales for furniture during the rest of the long vac."

She gulped. "What about the other house? Marcel is very fussy about his possessions and I have a certain obligation to see that it's all right there when he comes back."

"His possessions of course include you, but you must get used to the idea that never again will you live with him."

"I can't just walk out," she said firmly. "You have Judith to settle, too. We have to face up to the past if the future is to begin without recriminations. I love you, Robert. I want to live with you forever but I have to be easy in my mind before I build a nest."

"You were serious when you said you wanted a child?"

"Not just *a* child. I could have that with Marcel; I want *our* children, laughing, relaxed and noisy, with red hair."

He gazed at the ceiling, his hands behind his head on the hard pillow. "I wouldn't give Judith a baby. In my heart I knew that I would find you again, and I couldn't make ties that would bind me to her forever with a family I didn't want."

"But you do like children?"

"I shall love ours, with your dark eyes and hair and quick-silver changes of mood." They drowsed in a warm well of content until Antonia shivered and tried to find a way under the duvet on which they lay. "I'll go now," he whispered. "Sleep well, and no ghosts. I promise that everything will be fine."

He folded his side of the duvet over her like a sleeping bag, keeping his warmth and his smell next to her as she slept.

151

Chapter Nine

The fresh flowers in the wide crystal bowl on the library table showed that Mrs Regan had been in during the day. There was a drop of water on one of the leaves and most of the buds were tight. Antonia looked about her and the flowers did little to mask the unreality of her homecoming. Everything, as usual, was very clean, and magazines and books that were beyond Mrs Regan's limits of tidy initiative sat in staid piles, the bindings in perfect apposition and the covers smooth.

Antonia picked up two copies of *Good Housekeeping* and let them slide to the floor, but the influence of the room was too much and she picked them up again and replaced them carefully. How had this place ever seemed to be her home? The thick, embossed wallpaper, chosen by Marcel and matched carefully with the drapes and covers, were not hers. The highly polished furniture, valuable and hideous, was not in sympathy with the woman who liked light and shade dappling the carpet and no heavy wodges of solid shadow.

The silver letter tray was well to the front of her desk, as if reproaching her for her absence and she picked up the top envelope. Another invitation to a formal dinner in one week's time. At least that was a function she could miss. She made a note to reply with regrets and then wondered why she was bothering. The sky wouldn't fall in if she left it unanswered and the dinner would go on without them. It would be taken for granted that the invitation hadn't been received and that Antonia was in South America with her husband, like a dutiful wife. She crossed out the memo and opened the rest of the letters.

Marcel was back in camp, wondering why he had received no word from her, and asked for an immediate reply. He expressed concern about her pregnancy but didn't say that he missed her. He mentioned one or two of the team, and praised the work that Gerda had done, saying that she was intelligent and as keen as any of the men, strong and a good companion. She turned the page back and saw that he had referred to Gerda at least four times. 'Please, Antonia,' he wrote. 'Let me know at once how you are as this is very important to me. I know that you must be pregnant but I would like a confirmation of the fact.'

Antonia smiled. In the past, Marcel had ignored the possibility of children but now, having decided he wanted an heir to match him in looks and probably in temperament, she could sense the growing obsession that everything must be as he wished, as he ordered, but there was something more in his urgency that as yet she couldn't fathom.

Alone on a stony ridge, away from all the comfort he held so dear, Marcel might well become paranoic about his desire for a child stamped in his own image. She shivered. He must feel frustrated that he couldn't manage to have the baby without her help! His child could be used as a weapon against her if she ever tried to leave him, and would make her submit to everything he wanted in the future, binding her to him with no hope of escape.

To be in control of her reproductive system was important and Antonia blessed the headache pills that Marcel had mistaken for contraceptives. I am independent, she decided. He can't do anything more to me now, but when the telephone rang she jumped back as if Marcel had read her thoughts and was coming home.

She let it ring for half a minute and then raised the receiver slowly, hoping that it wasn't Robert. She needed time to wander through the rooms and to let the emptiness imprint on her before Robert's deep voice brought warmth to dispel the shadows and make her smile at the expensive luxury of the house.

"Antonia! How are you?"

"Bruce? How nice to hear from you. I've just got back from France and I haven't even unpacked. I hope this is a social call?" She smiled to herself.

"Is everything all right?"

"Fine, Dr Marden! Did you think I might have food poisoning after all that lovely French seafood and wine?"

"You managed to eat well?"

"It was super." She could hear herself talking as she did at a party, with all the bright responses and superlatives that meant nothing and which she despised even when she found them useful. "The class was quite bright and the weather perfect. I have a lovely tan and I think I put on a few ounces."

"Don't overdo it: the eating, I mean. We don't want you overweight, do we?"

"Stop being twee, Bruce." She couldn't hide her sudden irritation. "I may be alone but I'm not the little woman who needs buttering up because her husband is away. I don't even need to borrow a cup of sugar."

"Ah! Do I detect a hint of irritation? Not getting depressed, are we? Need a boost to get you over the psychological barrier of slim young thing turning into earth mother?"

She laughed her relief. "Oh, I forgot. You think I'm pregnant."

"Well, you are, aren't you?"

"Sorry to disappoint you, but no."

"But Marcel said that you were. He was certain."

"He might be but nature thought otherwise." For God's sake, leave it there, she wanted to say.

"My dear Antonia. Are you terribly disappointed?"

"As I never expected to be pregnant, how can I be disappointed? I've been on the Pill for the past year or so. You should know that. You prescribed the stuff."

"At these times, women get odd ideas," he said gently. "Better come down to the surgery tomorrow with a specimen. Marcel was very, very sure of this. We'll run a test."

"I'll have to leave it until I finish my period," she said sweetly. "We don't want a contaminated specimen, do we?"

"Then you really aren't pregnant?"

"Marcel thought he'd made me conceive but he was wrong. For once, my husband was wrong and didn't get what he wanted, and I shall have great pleasure in telling him that his plan didn't come off."

"I see," he said, in a tone that showed he didn't understand at all. "I'm really sad about this. You and Marcel are quite the best example of a married couple that I know. I'd hate to think you wanted children and couldn't have them. We could do tests," he suggested.

"I didn't want the child that Marcel planned so stop talking as if I had a tragic miscarriage. I'm well and happier than I've been for years and I'm not pregnant."

"Marcel is going to be very disappointed." She sensed that he considered her far too flip about the whole affair.

"What do you suggest? Shall I go out and find someone to make me preg just to please my husband?" She laughed and put the phone down gently, ignoring his anxious bleats.

She reached for notepaper and started 'Dear Marcel,' then put down her pen. What shall I write? 'Mother doing fine but no little stranger on the way yet?' 'Bad luck you flushed my headache pills down the loo instead of the real thing?' No, I can't put that on paper, she thought. There were no words she could write just now that grew out of the disgust she felt for the man who had tricked her so much in the past and had thought he had done so again. He'll bloody well have to wait, she decided and tore up the sheet of paper.

She unpacked and the clothes that she had folded carefully for the visit to France tumbled out in an expensive heap on the bedspread. The soiled cotton skirts and tops, stuffed into a plastic bag, went into the linen basket and she looked at the unsoiled clothes in wonder. Did I ever wear that? She held up a formal suit of dull grey silk that would have been good in a luxury hotel with Marcel, but not in a simple French auberge.

The silk shirts were fine and her own choice, in colours that she liked, but Marcel had a habit of bringing home clothes that he wanted her to wear on certain occasions so that he had a perfectly dressed wife in tow. Systematically, she went through her entire wardrobe, making piles of what she wanted to keep, the Marcel efforts and the clothes that she could pass on to Mrs Regan and her inexhaustible supply of relatives, who she vowed were all exactly the same size as Mrs Lambert, and wasn't that lucky?

She packed two suitcases and put the other clothes back in the wardrobe to clear the bed and the floor. The dressing-gown she had worn the last time that Marcel had forced her into bed and made violent love to her, she dropped into the waste bin, smiling as she imagined Mrs Regan's shocked cry as she rescued it and put it into her own capacious ditty bag. The picture of Mrs Regan wearing it for her Bert was too much and when the phone rang Antonia was still laughing.

"Hello, darling. You sound cheerful."

"Robert! Yes, I am. I've thrown out a lot of clothes and packed some things."

"Does that mean you are ready to come here?" he asked eagerly.

"Not yet. I have a lot to do and letters to write and I can't do that if you are around. Marcel is getting restive because he hasn't heard from me and the local medic was panting on the phone ready to give me extra vitamins and to listen to the foetal heartbeat."

"Sure you haven't flipped?"

"No, Robert my love. Under all this panic I'm happy. I don't yet know how I'll get away from Marcel, but coming back here convinced me, if I needed any convincing, that I could never live here again with him, even for another week."

"I'll have the cottage clear in ten days' time. Can you be ready?"

She gave a shuddering sigh. "I'll be there."

"You *are* upset?"

"It's hearing your voice. I've been here on my own and the chill of the place was getting to me. I must have been spiritually frozen when I was here with Marcel. Take no notice but go on talking." She wiped her eyes and concentrated on his voice, only half listening to the words. "What was that?"

"It might be nothing but I think you should watch the television news tonight. There's been a bit of trouble somewhere close to where Marcel is in South America. It may be miles away as it's such a big continent, but there are reports of a fall of rock where a group of geologists are working." The line was silent. "Antonia?"

"I'm here. I'll watch," she said. "Can you give me your number and I'll ring you tonight after the news."

She scribbled the number on the pad and added his initials.

"You will be all right?" he asked. "Do you want me to come down to you?"

"No, not here. I never want to see you in this house, Robert. I shall leave with memories of my life with Marcel and then I can leave easily, but not if you bring fresh memories to dim the influence he has on this house."

She finished tidying her room, noting that she needed a fresh bar of soap on the vanity unit. The towels in Marcel's bathroom needed changing and she pushed them into the linen basket and wrote a note for Mrs Regan to start up the washing machine as soon as she came in for her morning's work. How many more times will I do this? she wondered.

She inspected the contents of the fridge and found that Mrs Regan had filled it with good fresh food, so she prepared a meal, recalling with a smile that Robert had remembered that she made good curry back at the university, when the other students brought ingredients and they fed their friends, and everyone for miles could smell the pungent spices. No curry here as Marcel hated the smell and she could eat it only when they went out to dine, but she resolved to buy a dark earthenware pot when she was with Robert and they could revel in spicy food when the urge took them.

Mrs Regan will wonder what is happening when I leave, Antonia thought. She'd be glad to have the house to herself with little work to do, and if the neighbours were telling the truth, entertaining her own friends here whenever the Lamberts were away, but always keeping the house ready for their occupation at a day's notice. In ten days' time Mrs Regan would have the place to herself until Marcel returned. Ten days! Antonia took a tray of food and a glass of dry white wine into the sitting room and bent to switch on the television.

The steak was delicious and Antonia settled back to enjoy it with her shoes kicked off and the breeze from the open window stirring her hair. I'll watch the night later, she thought, and smell the late scents on the terrace. At no time did she feel tempted to ring a friend. Other women would raise the phone as soon as they returned from a holiday, but there was no one person living near who she wanted to call. All our friends are Marcel's, she realised. Friends and neighbours with whom we have formed a kind of casual warmth but who would not care if Marcel and I broke up. A few surprised shrugs maybe, a little amusement, but nothing to ruffle the smoothness of their lives. The women would think her a fool to leave someone as handsome and charming as Marcel, and turning her back on all that his wealth gave her would make them even more surprised. They saw only the sunlight and had no idea of the hidden rocks.

The last lines of a situation comedy faded into a roar of canned laughter, and colours merged with fresh music as the programmes changed and the familar run-in to the news began. Antonia paused in the doorway, the empty dishes in her hand. Robert wanted her to watch, although she was convinced that she would see nothing about Marcel, so she put the dishes on the work surface in the kitchen and hurried back, the wine bottle and a bowl of fruit in her hands.

There was a report of a mugging in a country lane, the rescue of a boy from a cliff-face, and the rumours of another royal romance, with poor-quality photographs that proved nothing. It was typical of any summer night on the news during the silly season, until the camera showed a high ridge of mountains that could not be in England or any part of America that Antonia had visited.

The luxury camp, with huge caravans and new tents were there as Marcel had described and shown in the photographs he had sent home to be given to his friends. Antonia stared but Marcel was not there in the picture. The reporter, wearing a very new bush jacket, was talking to a statuesque blonde woman wearing a very tight shirt, and trousers that clung like a second skin to the slightly solid but shapely thighs. That's Gerda, Antonia thought, so Marcel must be there somewhere. She looked at the full lips and bold eyes and knew that Gerda had expertise apart from her academic qualifications.

A fall of rock had destroyed most of the work done during the previous months before the experts arrived to bore and blast further. Antonia watched and listened but the news was vague and there was no mention of bad casualties, although Gerda said that there had been a few accidents. No, she couldn't allow those injured to be interviewed yet but she wanted everyone at home to know that the geologists were safe. Antonia thought that she looked directly into the camera as if talking to her, but Gerda would never think her worth considering and there were other relatives who might well be concerned.

Antonia poured more wine and took a small bunch of grapes, watching the rest of the news and feeling that she had seen just another educational film about geology that didn't touch her closely. The edge of danger made her curious but there had seemed to be no urgency, no sense of tragedy as the calm blonde woman gave the sparse details.

"We have just received further reports from South America," an announcer broke in later. "We now know that the accident occurred two days ago and we can bring you more details." The camp was shown again with a long trestle table, behind which sat members of the team. Antonia smiled. Two men had fresh white bandages on their heads and one had an arm in plaster. She gasped. Marcel reclined on a camp bed, covered with a light blanket, with a very romantic bandage round his head but no other visible signs of injury. His deep tan made him almost as dark as the local servants hovering in the background and, by contrast, Gerda, who stood by his side, seemed even more fair. Marcel wore no shirt and looked like an elegant and healthy ox.

Gerda seemed to act as the main spokesperson and said firmly that the men had been seen and treated by an eminent surgeon who was a member of the party and that they required no outside aid. Mr Lambert would not be returning to the UK, as they expected him to be well enough to proceed with his work in a few days' time. "We have much work to do and the programme will be more lengthy than we envisaged," she said.

She stood close to the bed and smiled at the man on it, and Antonia saw that she could hardly keep her hands away from him. "Of course he won't come home. He'll have every kind of tender loving care there!" Antonia said, but wondered why he was lying on a bed. If a leg was in plaster, he would show it and make the most of the dramatic wounded warrior bit.

The camera swung closer to his face and Marcel looked far more tense than Antonia had at first realised. He smiled. "We were lucky," he said with false modesty. "As soon as we heard the warning sounds of the rocks splitting, of course we knew exactly what to do to avoid the main fall. This," he said, touching the bandage, "and the other injuries, were caused by flying rocks." He moved slightly and winced, and Gerda stepped between him and the camera, but he waved her away.

"Have you managed to get in touch with your families?" the reporter asked.

"No," Marcel said firmly. "I refused to allow my wife to be upset until we knew the extent of the damage both to ourselves and to our important work. A shock like this when my dear wife is expecting our first child might be very bad for her pregnancy." Antonia was fascinated. Gerda put a hand on his bare shoulder and it looked at home and familiar there, as if in loving relationship with the rest of his body. "I shall remain at the base camp to organise the team until I am fit again but one of my colleagues will have to go back to the UK, as he is no longer mobile with a very heavy plaster on his leg."

"Will you need a replacement?" the reporter asked.

"No, Dr Gerda Baum will take his place. She is highly qualified and understands what is needed."

"I'll bet she does!" said Antonia. She wanted to laugh, and wondered if this was the night when she should get really sloshed. Marcel wouldn't be home as soon as expected! It might be weeks and weeks or even months before she had to face him. She took a last look at the scene before switching off and had the satisfaction of seeing Gerda dwindle to a tiny dot in the darkening screen. I can shut this place up and go to Robert as soon as I am ready, she decided. If I have my life organised before Marcel comes back he can't touch me.

"Did you see it?" Robert asked half an hour later when she telephoned. "Are you okay?"

"Wonderful! I celebrated the fact that Marcel can't come back yet and I think I'm a bit lightheaded."

"You don't feel an impulse to rush to his side?"

"Don't sound so anxious. It was like watching a stranger."

"What about the dear pregnant wife?"

"I have no intention of telling him anything. I have not said I'm pregnant and I have not said I'm not."

"He'll have to know. Wouldn't it be easier to write and tell him and finish with him completely now?"

"I'd like to do that, Robert, but there will be lots to settle first and things that I can't avoid. You have the same problems with Judith, I'm sure."

"Nothing like your set up, but I agree that I shall have to see Judith to tie up loose ends. Promise me you will come here on Thursday week?"

"I promise. I'm with you now, except for my body."

"I could do with that right now," he said dryly.

"Ring me tomorrow, please?" Antonia sighed. "If only it

wasn't so messy. I want to leave here now, post the keys through the letterbox and go without a backward glance."

"Not long now and then we shall be together for always."

"Always," she whispered and, "Always," she said again as she picked up her book and went upstairs. She stopped at the door of the master bedroom and switched on the light. It was tidy after her onslaught earlier and the bed was smooth and impersonal. She switched off the light and went to the smaller of the guest rooms, which she had furnished in soft blues and turquoise when Marcel was away. He had smiled indulgently when he saw it and said it was fine so long as he didn't have to sleep there.

She slipped under the soft duvet and read until the book dropped to the floor, and when the telephone woke her the light was still on.

"Yes?" she said, her voice husky with sleep.

"Person to person call for Mrs Antonia Lambert."

"Yes, I am she," said Antonia, sitting up straight and brushing the hair from her eyes. She couldn't see the face of her alarm clock but knew it must be in the small hours.

"Antonia?" Marcel's voice was clear and so close that the room seemed to cringe back to avoid him.

"Marcel? Are you all right?" It was ridiculous. She had seen him on television and knew he was fine, but there was nothing more she could think of to say. She recovered. "I saw the interview on television but before that I knew nothing about the accident." That was better. She felt more composed and was saying the right words. "You said that you might have

165

to stay on for some weeks?" Her heart pounded. What if he had rung to tell her that he was coming home now? Oh, God, don't let him come home now! "Are you in pain?" she asked.

"Not now. I have a good team who are looking after me. Our medic is first class and we do have our own well-equipped surgery unit," he added, as if telling it to a five-year-old.

"Gerda looked as if she had everything under control," Antonia said maliciously.

"Gerda? Oh, yes, very efficient, but I didn't phone all this way to talk about my team." He's embarrassed, she thought. Good!

"Randolph Heath is coming home," he went on. "He's the one with the broken leg and a badly sprained arm. He's a single man with no real home so I said that he could stay in our house while he is convalescing and having intensive physiotherapy as an outpatient."

"Why here? He isn't local. Isn't he from the north?"

"It's the best I could think of, and the least I could do for the poor chap. I know he likes you and it seemed right to suggest it."

"I thought you disliked him! At one time you said he was a womaniser who you would never leave alone with any female in your family for five minutes!"

"I was mistaken." His voice was cold. "He is a valuable member of the team and as such I have a responsibility to him. I'm afraid you'll have to bury your silly prejudices, Antonia, and try to make him feel at home." The line crackled. "He'll fly over next week but I'll cable the time later."

166

No goodbye, no sorry I got you up at this hour, and what was he saying? *My* prejudices? I liked Randolph when I was allowed anywhere near him. He was fun but Marcel steered me away as if he might be contaminated. She lay awake, wondering what Marcel had on his mind. Certainly Gerda, and probably something more. It wasn't until much later that she recalled that he had made no mention of the baby that he was so ready to talk about on television.

The softly lit room comforted her. I shall bring all my things in here until I leave, she decided. Randolph might as well spread himself in the main suite. If he comes after next Thursday I shall miss seeing him but I'll make sure he is comfortable and Mrs Regan will see that he has everything he needs. She yawned. Mrs Regan will get on well him as he does get a bit familiar and she likes that.

Chapter Ten

"But what will you do without him all that time, Mrs Lambert?"
Mrs Regan stood with one hand on her hip and wondered when
her employer would be likely to pass on the nice cotton blouse.
The skirt wasn't up to much, being the kind that Maureen Regan
could afford to buy for herself if she went abroad on a package
holiday, but the blouse was nice.

"He says that he may be away for at least three or four
months," Antonia said. Her voice shook as she dared to consider what life would be like for the rest of the summer and
well into the autumn. I'm a gross coward, she thought, but it
was wonderful to postpone any confrontation with Marcel. The
letter was still clutched in her hand, as if to prove to her that it
was true. She just couldn't believe it unless she read it aloud.
'The fall of rock completely obliterated an important seam and
the excavations have to start all over again.'

"Fancy that," Mrs Regan said with complete indifference.
"Can't they just dig another hole somewhere else? But I don't
know about these things." She smiled. If he was away life

would be easy; no parties with piles of dishes left for her to stack in the dishwasher, carpets to clean and rooms to make ready for odd guests. She made a mental note to ask her cousin to stay if Mrs Lambert took it into her head to join him. "I expect he misses you, Mrs Lambert. Don't you want to fly out to join him, especially as he's wounded?" she said, with an air of mild reproach. "Bert and me would be glad to sleep in and caretake for you again." It sounded like a carefully considered sacrifice. "We wouldn't mind, really we wouldn't."

"The house won't be empty, Mrs Regan." Antonia saw her disappointment. "I shall be here until next week and after that I have some teaching jobs I've accepted, when I'll stay at the university, but I don't go just yet."

"So you will be away some of the time?" Mrs Regan brightened. There would still be time for her relatives to visit her. "Just let me know dates and I'll have everything ready for when you come back," she offered generously. "You can come back and have a nice rest before you go away again."

Antonia smiled, knowing how her brain was working. "I'd give you plenty of warning," she said. Mrs Regan flushed. "It's all right, I've known for ages that you entertain your own friends while we are away and it doesn't worry me in the least. My husband doesn't know and I see no reason to tell him."

"You wouldn't ever tell him? Mr Lambert, I mean?"

"No, I value your service and loyalty far too much to do that. If you use the spare rooms that's up to you. I only mention it so that you know that he would be angry if he did find out, so you'll have to be careful."

"If you're going to be here, I shan't be able to have anyone in, so there will be nothing for him to find out."

Antonia referred to the letter again. "Mr Lambert spoke to me on the phone last night."

"All the way from Peru?"

"Yes, no expense spared and clear as a bell," Antonia said dryly. "He wanted to know if I'd seen the news bulletin and to reassure me that he was safe, but also to tell me that one of his team, a Mr Heath, was injured enough to make a return to England necessary. He has a fractured leg and a badly bruised arm which will need physiotherapy."

"What a drag to come back all this way. I thought that woman on the news said they had everything that a hospital could offer out there. Why couldn't they have his arm rubbed there?"

"I did wonder that myself," Antonia said slowly. "However, my husband wants him to come back and stay here for a while for as long as it takes to have treatment at the private hospital."

"Why here? He isn't local, is he? I remember Mr Heath coming here once. Nice looking man but a bit saucy, if you ask me." She sniffed. "Don't they have private hospitals where he lives?"

"I suppose so, but my husband feels responsible for him because the accident happened under his leadership, and as he has no wife or family – he was divorced a couple of years ago – he does need help." She frowned. "He's arriving next week, I think, but my husband will telephone again or send a cable with the exact date. Will you get the main suite ready for him, and I'll sleep in the blue room until I go away."

"You don't want to turn out of your nice room, Mrs Lambert."

"I have taken some of my things out and done a lot of sorting and Mr Heath will want space for his papers and belongings, so he might as well have that suite. He can work there and not mess up the study. You can lock up the rest of the house except for the breakfast room and the kitchen. I don't want him in my studio, either. It will be far less work for you if we keep him in one place, and I may be away for a few weeks at a time."

"That would be easier," Mrs Regan conceded. Her mind made rapid calculations. "If he's to stay all that time, would you mind if my daughter came one day a week to help, as I suppose he'll have to be fed as well and I'll have to cook for him."

"I'm glad you mentioned that. Come to my study and we'll work out a programme. I might not be here to check with you for some time, so I want to know that all expenses are met during that time."

It was working out better than she had thought possible. Randolph Heath could have the house to himself with Mrs Regan and her daughter to attend to his needs.

"I only saw him once, but what's he really like, Mrs Lambert?"

Antonia laughed. "You'll like him. Just be careful not to let your daughter fall for him. He's rather attractive and has a reputation as a womaniser."

"Is that why you are going away?" The dark eyes were shrewd. "Do you know him really well?"

"That's not the reason," Antonia said firmly. "I'd arranged to teach long before I heard that he was coming here. I don't think I've seen him for almost two years." She opened the rolltop desk. "Not my type at all."

"Not after Mr Lambert. Now he's what I call attractive." Antonia ignored the implied question. "We wondered when you might start a family," Mrs Regan said slyly.

"You never can tell," Antonia replied facetiously, then regretted what she had said as the woman glanced at her waistband, tightened by good French food and love. I really must go on a diet when I get to the cottage, she thought. I must have put on six or eight pounds. Happiness fat, her granny had called it. Every bride puts it on at first because she doesn't worry and she's happy; and I'm happy and feel married even if that can't as yet be publicly recognised.

"Go on, you can't fool me. We all saw the news and Mr Lambert saying that you were expecting. You'll have nice babies," Mrs Regan was saying. "My Sandra is good with little ones if you ever need a nanny."

"Let's cross that bridge when we come to it. It was a false alarm," Antonia said firmly. "Now, let's get down to business. I think I'll ask my lawyer to pay your weekly cheque until one of us returns for good. Make a list of everything you need and take it to the store where I have an account and they'll deliver the provisions. I'll ask the lawyer to pay all the bills and if your daughter works here, she must be paid separately, for tax purposes."

Mrs Regan looked uncertain. It would be better if she had

the handling of the buying, then she could have a few perks for herself, but she could think of nothing to say.

"Any questions?" Antonia asked.

"No, madam. Oh, there is one thing. I found your nice kimono in the waste bin. Did you mean to put it out for washing?"

"No, I've finished with it. Give it away if you want, and I've a few things that your daughter might like and some that you could wear." She laughed. "If Mr Lambert is away all the summer, you will be quite safe to wear them here." She had met her housekeeper in a neighbouring village wearing a dress that she had cast off and Mrs Regan had scuttled into a shop with a very red face to avoid being seen.

"Come and see if there's anything you like before I get rid of some clothes," Antonia said, and they went to the big wardrobe where the rejected garments were stored. Mrs Regan emerged from the bedroom after half an hour, flushed and excited with a case full of good designer clothes.

"I'll get you a nice lunch and then take these home," she said. "I'll be back later to cook dinner and to set you up for breakfast." She had hesitated over two finely pleated exquisite cotton dresses which hung from the shoulders with no restricting belt so that they were cool in very hot weather. "Are you sure about these?" she'd asked. "They are lovely and they'd do for maternity dresses. That's if you ever need them now." She sighed. "Pity about that, but I expect you don't want to be reminded."

"I wore them last year and frankly never really liked them."

Antonia didn't explain that it was the maternity look that she had found depressing.

"They'll be nice and cool to wear here and work in," Mrs Regan said. "With that loose fit, they'll be just right for me but I'll have to alter some of the others as some of your fitted things are a bit tight." She picked up the letters from the hall table. "What shall I do about letters? Do you want them sent on or will you be visiting Mr Heath and pick them up then?"

"That's a point. I don't know where I shall be taking classes at first. For some of the time I may be miles away or even abroad, so I think you'd better send them in charge of the professor of the art faculty at my old university. He knows what courses I shall be teaching and can send the letters on without delay. I may stay at the university and teach there in a series of adult education classes, but that has to be settled. The facilities for working there are good and I want to finish some paintings and sketches I started in France."

It all sounded cool and businesslike. She saw that Mrs Regan wasn't even listening. "I'll write his name on the pad in the hall by the phone so that you can deal with the letters as soon as they arrive. Now get off home and try on the clothes! I can see that I shall have no work done until you have shown them to your daughter."

Ten minutes later, Mrs Regan called to say that she was off. "There's a nice salad on the table, madam, and I've cleared the kitchen." Antonia walked slowly down to eat lunch, and decided to sit on the patio overlooking the quiet driveway at one side of the house, where Marcel had made no impression on the disorder and exuberance of the hydrangea bushes but had left them because they gave a lot of privacy. The sun was very bright and she had forgotten to bring sunglasses, so she left the salad on the table under a sun umbrella and went to fetch them with a book that she had half read.

She came back wearing the huge dark glasses behind which she hid her feelings when Marcel was in a rage or a bad mood and which allowed her to appear calm and unafraid. They made a blessed haven but didn't cut out the sudden flash of light she saw, and a movement at the end of the driveway. She frowned. Someone taking flash photographs? She shrugged. One of the neighbour's children probably had a new camera and was short of subjects, but she tilted the shady umbrella so that she was hidden from the driveway before starting her meal.

She stared down the driveway as she had second thoughts about the flashlight. It could be a reporter who wanted stolen pictures and who would add his own caption to the invented interview with the wife of the man involved in the rock fall in South America. I suppose the local papers would like an interview, she realised, and almost wished that she had agreed when a reporter rang to ask her to appear on the local radio news. An exclusive interview might protect her from furtive rustlings in the bushes and the telephone calls that asked when her baby was expected and had the news of her husband's escape from death upset her?

She settled down to read. Tomorrow, the fact that a local man had been injured by a rock fall hundreds of miles away would be stale news and just another silly season, Loch Ness monster tale, soon forgotten as fresh drama filled the papers. The book was less interesting than she had supposed and she thought about the reporter. He was certainly persistent and she hated the feeling that someone was watching her. The expected ring at the doorbell didn't come and she began to read again. He would phone later and take her off guard, she decided. The engine of a car started along the road where there was a hedge but no driveway, as if someone had parked in a hidden spot off the main road to eat sandwiches, and half a minute later she saw a caterpillar-green old Dyane move slowly past the main gate.

Only birds now interrupted the peace and she had never found the distant murmur of traffic bothersome. She leaned back on the sun lounger and the book was heavy on her chest. Another few days and she would be with Robert in the cottage, their cottage, where he would be waiting, warm and loving and eager for her. The daily phone calls were her salvation but she wanted his nearness, the smell and feel of him and the fleeting laughter behind his tenderness. She wanted his body as she had never wanted a man until now, and needed his heaviness pressing her down and making them one, bringing body and mind together in desperate satisfaction.

The telephone was ringing and the sun was slanting under the shade onto her face. Rainbows of light and darkness came and went as she tried to focus and wondered why it was dark when the sun was shining. She took off the dark glasses and stumbled to her feet, cursing her afternoon nap which had done nothing to relax her. The ringing made her hurry, and she wished now that she had taken the cordless extension into the garden with her. As she reached the study door, the ringing stopped. What did it matter? Robert never rang at this hour and whoever it was could ring again.

She smiled as she saw Mrs Regan hurrying up the drive. She was wearing the dark red cotton dress, and the pleating and good fabric flowed over her thick waist, concealing it and making her look far more lissom than she could claim to be.

"No need to rush," Antonia said. "I'm not going out tonight and I don't want a heavy meal as it's so hot. Just a chop and salad will do very well. I think I shall work in my study for an hour and then make notes for my lectures." She saw that Mrs Regan was angry and not just hot. "What's wrong?"

"That man! Has he been round here again?"

"What man? Calm down and tell me."

"I said to my Sandra the other day that a man had been hanging round here. He tried to talk to me the other day. Followed me to the supermarket when I left here and tried to take my photo."

"You must have a secret admirer," Antonia said, and laughed. "You should feel flattered."

"I think he's a villain looking this place over before he breaks in," Mrs Regan said, with heavy emphasis. "Casing the joint!"

"If that was so, he wouldn't advertise the fact that he was interested," Antonia replied. "I think he's a reporter. I refused to be interviewed after the accident and he's trying to get a few pictures, and possibly a story. Don't worry about him, Mrs Regan. He's only doing his job as he sees it."

"Funny way to earn a living if you ask me. If my Bert was killed and they put a microphone under my nose and asked how I felt, I'd tell them where to put it," she said.

"He was here at lunch time. Was that when you saw him?"

"It must be the same man. He was there this morning while you were indoors and I went out to the shops. I forgot to tell you when we were busy clearing out the clothes. Large as life he was, sitting on the wall, dangling a great big camera from his neck, enough to give him round shoulders. He had the cheek to ask if I was Mrs Lambert."

"What did you say?" Antonia was fascinated.

"I haven't time to waste on men like him and I told him so. I said it was a pity he had nothing better to do than sit on other people's walls and that it was no concern of his *who* I was."

"I don't need a minder with you around," Antonia said. There were times when Mrs Regan put on a falsely refined voice and sounded as if she was imitating a royal princess. She now reverted to her normal voice with the relief of someone easing off tight shoes.

"Cheeky monkey!" she said. "He'll get nothing from me."

"Well done. He may take your hint and go away after easier prey," Antonia said hopefully. The phone rang again. "Would you answer it? If it's your young man, tell him I'm not interested in interviews and that's final."

Mrs Regan fled to the phone and Antonia could hear her irate and pseudo-cultured tones once more. She smiled and went to the studio to collect her books and papers and to sort out canvases that she wanted to take away with her. If anyone could send the reporter packing it was Mrs Regan, who now called up the stairs. "I sent him off with a flea in his ear. He won't ring again, I don't think. I hope you don't mind, Mrs Lambert, but I was rather rude," she added with satisfaction.

"Good for you! Did he say which paper he represented?"

"I didn't ask."

Antonia hummed to herself as she packed a large folder and wondered if the drawings made in France would come to life once she was settled in the cottage, as she had no intention of starting new work until she was safely away. Soon, she would be where no reporter would bother to look for her for a run-of-the-mill interview. She mildly wondered if he was from the local evening paper or one of the county glossies. This wasn't really their style. A good magazine would have contacted her politely by letter, with none of the brash intrusion of the popular press. She shrugged. The incident was finished and was one over which she need lose no sleep.

The next phone call she knew instinctively was from Robert. "Hello," she said and waved away Mrs Regan, who had come from the kitchen ready for battle. She hurried back to the white sauce that might curdle if left and shut the kitchen door. "That was Mrs Regan but she's gone now," Antonia explained. "It may be better if you ring a bit later after she's gone home. Not that it really matters but she's a nosy woman and I want to keep this to ourselves for a bit longer, my love."

"Tomorrow I'll ring later," Robert agreed, and knew that

Antonia didn't want her housekeeper gloating over Madam's bit on the side, as she would label their love, reducing it to sex and nothing more. "I've finished the ceilings," he said. "Can you fancy a white-haired husband? I didn't paint cupids as I dreaded to think what colour I'd be."

"The cottage is hardly the Sistine Chapel," Antonia said. "Stick to white; you always did splash colour about." She pictured his face after a hard day at work for her, tired but human and caring and beloved.

"It's nearly all done. I'm ready to receive you at any time, darling."

"So am I. I can come in two days' time." She told him what arrangements she had made for Mrs Regan and the house. "If I can walk out knowing that everything will run as smoothly as if I didn't exist, Marcel will have no cause to complain that I walked out on him without doing my duty."

"And when he does come back?"

"He can do as he pleases. By that tine I shall be so used to being with you that I shall have built up a wall of courage. You give me strength, Robert. I went through everything here and it was as if I cleared away after someone died. In a way, I have died. The Antonia Lambert who lived here is dead."

"Long live the new-born Antonia," he said. "In a little while I shall hold you in my arms. Did you know that our bedroom looks out on the poplar avenue? With the windows wide open we shall hear what they are saying."

She told him about the reporter and made him laugh about Mrs Regan. "Must go," she said as she heard the kitchen door open The blast of music followed Mrs Regan into the hall and across to the dining room, where she laid a solitary place setting with the best glass and silver, as if nothing was too good for her generous employer. "I'll ring you later. I forgot to tell you something but it will have to wait now." The advent of Randolph Heath seemed quite unimportant.

As she ate the sole mornay and sipped a glass of white wine, Antonia pondered about Randolph. It was so out of character for Marcel to offer help of this nature, to encourage her to be with a man for whom he had expressed dislike and distrust where women were concerned. Randolph, of all people? Living in the same house as Antonia, by kind permission of a pathologically jealous husband? It was as if Marcel didn't care what happened, or even wanted something to occur between them.

A month ago, if Marcel had discovered his wife having a cup of tea in the local Olde Worlde Café with Randolph, he would have accused her of gross infidelity and been so furious that she would have to have done anything he asked to placate him. It was bizarre. Maybe, she thought, Randolph had threatened to sue after the accident and this was the only way that Marcel could show the world that they were good friends.

It worried her, niggling like an untrimmed hangnail until she was alone and could telephone the cottage. Robert was quiet while she told him about Randolph and read the extract from Marcel's letter concerning him. "I just don't understand," she said at last. She also mentioned the reporter again and the fact that she was uneasy knowing that he had spied on her from the drive. "I think I'd better let Mrs Regan be interviewed as me.

He does seem to think she is Mrs Lambert and he's becoming very persistent." She tried to laugh but sensed that Robert was growing anxious.

"Come tomorrow," he said. "I have a feeling that you ought to be with me."

"I shall be with you the day after tomorrow," she said.

"Come now! I don't trust that man. To announce to the world that you are pregnant might possibly be the wishful thinking of a man who has never been thwarted and thinks that he can achieve anything that he wants desperately enough, as he seems to want a child, but would any sane man leave his wife alone in a house with a man of Heath's reputation?" He gave a short laugh. "He doesn't include you in the services, does he? If you are pregnant he might think it doesn't matter what you do. From what you have told me, anything is possible in that perverted mind, like the saying: 'Nobody misses a slice from a cut cake,' and he may even enjoy being a mental voyeur!"

"No, you've got it wrong. You don't understand him. Do you remember James Fahmi, the Anglo-Egyptian who was in Normandy? In many ways he shared Marcel's philosophy that a wife must be pure and, like Caesar's wife, above suspicion."

"Which makes this arrangement even more suspect, as if he wants you . . . defiled. Come tomorrow, early, and never go back."

"I was going to welcome Randolph and make him feel at home," she began. "He arrives tomorrow."

"*No*! I want you out of that house. Start as soon as you've had breakfast. Can you pack the car tonight?

"But Robert!"

"Please, Antonia. I can feel my skin crawling. I know you must leave that place."

She could feel his tension and almost hear the fast beating of his heart. His mood was contagious and she shook with something akin to panic. "I'll come, Robert. Promise me that everything will be all right? If I leave now, there will never be a turning back, not ever." The claustrophobic security of the years with Marcel had been safe and ordered. Some of the times had been good. She looked at all that she had taken for granted and shivered.

It was a risk, giving it up to make a new life, having to consider expense carefully, after accounts at several leading stores and any clothes she wished to buy.

"Don't," Robert said gently. "I can picture you now. You are biting your lower lip and trying not to cry. I love you. I want you more than I've wanted any other person in my life. I've never stopped loving you. The rest will come if we really need it, unless you have been cushioned for so long that you can no longer live for the moment and just plan for a future when we may have spare time and money."

"I know," she said. "You'll have to help me, Robert. I feel so churned up that I can hardly think."

"We'll be together," he said. "We might even find that we have more to live for now that we have both suffered. Come to me tomorrow and we'll go and choose a bed. We can't sleep together on the bed I'm using. It would collapse."

She laughed, the tremor in her hands fading. "You have all

the right priorities. I do have some things of my own from my grandmother. I refused to get rid of them when Marcel dismissed them as sentimental rubbish and I've arranged for them to be delivered from store next week. I'd forgotten how much there was, so we can camp in the cottage until it all arrives." Her voice grew stronger and eager and she heard him let out a deep breath very slowly. "Robert?" she said. "Were you very worried?"

"I thought you might not come. Today, I spilled a whole can of emulsion on the floor and I was afraid that it was a sign that I would be clumsy with you and that nothing I did could make you leave him."

"We can cover the floor with matting and dhurries," she said, suddenly calm. "Expect me about noon tomorrow. I'll make an early start."

Her packing now became urgent. She wrote notes about almost everything that was routine in the house, a polite letter to Randolph Heath saying how much she regretted not being there to meet him, and full instructions for Mrs Regan, adding the address of the head of the arts faculty as her forwarding address.

It was right to leave now. In two weeks she was due to teach at Bangor and it would be nice to leave the cottage habitable for Robert as he also had committments at that time in the university. She folded a skirt and gazed into space. They would be together, but always there would be gaps while they went about their own business. It would be good and she would feel secure even when Robert was far away. When Marcel went away she was still aware of his disapproval and latent violence hanging over her, as if he could see what she was doing. She knew that after each trip he asked Mrs Regan questions and telephoned nice boring friends to make sure that she had been in touch with them, keeping tabs on all she did.

With Robert, she could hurry back and they would share their experiences and even though they were deeply in love, they could still enjoy work and the freedom of their individual jobs. What had Gibran said? 'Let there be spaces in your togetherness and let the winds of Heaven dance between you.'

It was midnight and the lights in the main suite blazed from the windows as Antonia pushed the last suitcase onto the half-landing. She went down to the kitchen and made coffee, cut a sandwich and took it back upstairs to her bureau as she wanted to add to the notes that she had to leave. Randolph might need Mrs Regan in the house for a few nights at first, if he was very incapacitated, but she knew that he was coming by taxi from the airport, so he wasn't an ambulance case. She chewed the end of her pen, wondering if she had forgotten anything. She added the telephone number and name of her doctor and closed the lid of the desk.

"I'm leaving," she told the room. "Even if it doesn't work out for Robert and me, I shall have no regrets and I'm never, never coming back." Saying it gave the situation substance and she turned back to the desk, taking a sheet of her best notepaper and sitting very straight on her seat, like a girl taking an unwelcome examination in a subject far beyond her capabilities. She took a deep breath and began her letter to Marcel. It was short and cool and left nothing uncertain.

'I have decided that we are not suited for a lifetime together. I am conscious of all that you have contributed to our marriage and for some of it I am grateful but I would like a divorce, Marcel, for your sake as well as mine. You need a woman who can take a part in your professional life. I can never do that, so I am leaving to pick up the threads of my old career.

If proceedings are started before you get back, it might lessen the hurt for both of us. Believe me when I say that this is an irrevocable decision on my part, and even if you do not consent to divorce, I shall not be here when you return. I have accepted teaching jobs and hope to be completely independent of you from now on.'

She folded the letter and addressed the envelope, checked the weight and the required postage and put it downstairs ready to post. I'm glad I kept this until now, she thought. It gives me time to get away before he reads it. I can tell Robert now that I have written to Marcel and that will make him feel more secure. The tension in their last phonecall had convinced her that she must not only make her decisions but be seen to do so, leaving no possible door open through which she could return to her old life.

She drank more coffee and turned out the lights in the main suite. It was after two in the morning but she wasn't sleepy.

She checked her handbag and purse, relieved to see that her personal bank account was healthy. She smiled sadly. In many ways Marcel was generous, and because he wanted her to depend on him entirely, he had refused to allow her to use any of the money left to her by her parents and grandparents. She found that it had accumulated. It provided a safe reserve for emergencies and made her truly independent. Even with Robert, she wanted to be free financially at first, able to draw out her own money without using funds that should be used for their mutual expenses. I may want to buy Robert presents and I can do so freely.

She stopped to think of the other decision left to her and knew that she had made no mention of the fact that she was not pregnant. Marcel will come back believing that I am at least four or five months pregnant. She sighed. It just wasn't important enough to her to tear up a perfectly good envelope and add that information as a postscript. He could be told later when the first letter had sunk in.

Half past three and the first birds awoke. In another four hours, the traffic would build up and she knew by the warmth of the early dawn that another hot day lay ahead. I could go now, she thought. I can drive in the cool, empty streets and lanes and be with Robert for breakfast. Her eyes sparkled, imagining his surprised delight. She locked her bureau and took the key down to Marcel's study, looked back at the neat rooms and piled her luggage into the back of the car.

A cat dropped down from a wall and stretched his long grey shape over the stones. I can have a cat of my own, or a dog.

A cat would be better if Robert and I are away, and Adrian is a cat person; his wife has three. They would look after ours and see that they were never neglected. A Burmese, with beautiful lustrous eyes and a throaty purr, that would pose for Robert, or an alley cat of unknown origins that would come to them obsequiously at first when he was rescued and then take over and permit them to own him. Antonia chuckled. It would be fun and wonderful when they had a child. She would feel complete.

The road widened and followed the hills, narrowed and went between tall hedgerows that grew more and more familiar. She saw the village that lay a few miles from the campus, and over the silvered rose of dawn she glimpsed the avenue of poplars and home.

Chapter Eleven

Marcel Lambert turned on the narrow bed and shivered. He had felt the fever mounting as the television cameras were on him but the heavy doses of anti-malaria pills and some painkilling tablets that Gerda had insisted that he needed, made him seem normal when the interview was in progress, but they had worn off and he had refused to take more. He felt stiff, but the bruising of his legs and groin hurt less than yesterday and the bleeding had stopped.

"You have slept?" Gerda asked. He reached for the cool hand that smoothed his wet brow with a tissue, and kissed her wrist.

"Much better," he lied. She sat on the edge of the bed and he saw her through a haze.

"Not better," she said and pursed her lips. "Maybe you should go back to UK?"

"No," he said vehemently. "We have everything we need here and I can't leave you, Gerda." He knew an almost desperate desire to please her and to be well just because she wanted him to be. Gerda was the most positive woman he had ever met and it was a novel experience for him to be a slave instead of an enslaver.

She moved away from his touch. "You are wet. I will sponge you and the paramedic will come to dress your wound." He watched the taut buttocks under the tight jeans as she walked out into the sunshine and he winced. The portable electric fan hitched to the generator outside the tent sent wafts of her scent back to him and he closed his eyes, willing his painful body not to want her, but even now, he knew that he desired her more than any woman he had known.

Antonia was a ghost, a woman from the past who was to fulfill the necessary function of providing him with a son who would be a second Marcel Lambert, but he recalled her dark hair without emotion and her features were unclear in his memory. She had learned to be good in bed in a passive, defensive way that goaded him into scarcely veiled contempt, never matching his desire, and cringing away from the edge of violence for which his sexuality craved.

He wanted Gerda but knew that she would finish the job she had started before looking in to see him and would come back in her own time, keeping him waiting and returning with a bowl of cool water and a sponge and the tantalising touch of her strong hands. The camp doctor had taken swabs of the blood from his genitals and gone to make tests and to find more antibiotics, unsure if the fever was infection or malaria, as the glands in his loins were swollen and hard and very bruised.

"I can do you now," she said, and smiled. "You could have

better treatment from the paramedic if you think I keep you waiting too long," she added and set the bowl down on the table. "He can do the dressings."

"Please, come here."

She laughed softly, showing perfect teeth gleaming between full red lips. Her breasts brushed against him as he reached up and seized her hand and she let their warmth stay with him for a few seconds. "I must wash you and then after your dressing you can lie in the shade out there." She peeled off his soaking shirt and he gasped with pleasure as the cool water eased away the risen temperature. She washed him all over except for where the skin was covered with gauze and adhesive plaster, with an impersonal touch as if she bathed a child. Everything she did was efficient with no time for sentimental dalliance or a kiss in passing and no visible change in her manner when she washed round the dressing on his groin. She was the perfect professional in everything she attempted. She had good degrees, making her an invaluable member of the team and now, if she had a slim white dress and a nurse's cap, she could easily be the perfect nurse. Marcel was quiet, subdued by his weakness and worried about his injuries, aware that Gerda was about to say something vital, but she remained silent.

"Darling Gerda," he said with the charm that usually got him what he wanted. It had seldom let him down and had won him a wife once, when he needed a woman to mould to his desired image, with the long-term conviction that Antonia would become the perfect hostess and the perfect mother for his children. A son would be born, with dark eyes and as handsome as his parents.

Gerda smiled slightly and picked up the bowl of water. She walked away with it and Marcel felt the sweat forming again, not because of the fever but because he was aware that she might not want him now if his sexual prowess was in jeopardy. After passionate sex, he had told her about Antonia being pregnant and she had laughed, saying that she never wanted to bear children but was content to be his lover and let his wife have babies.

When she took him to bed, she had left him breathless and totally bemused by her almost depraved lovemaking, but when he had gone to her, hot for sex the following night, she had pushed him away as if he violated a nun. He recalled the wet, red lips and the mockery of her eyes. "I've changed my mind," she said. "I want to marry you sooner than I planned." The message was obvious. Take me when you are free but until then, you burn.

She came back and helped him into a clean shirt and the paramedic dressed his injuries, leaving him comfortable for the first time. The fever was less now and when they were alone, Marcel took Gerda's hand and kissed it. His smile was boyish and one-sided and she bent to kiss his cheek.

"I love you so much," he said. "Sit with me for a while?"

"You really feel stronger?" He nodded and knew that this was true, and he needed no painkillers. "Then you must work," she said calmly. She helped him onto a lounger and put her arms round him from behind before pushing up the back rest. Her arms pressed him to the pillowy glory of her bosom. "Soon we will play a little as the doctor says that you will be able to perform again, but now we must arrange for the future." He frowned, unused to any woman giving orders and feeling like an intelligent geriatric put to doing remedial basketwork.

She felt his tension and bent to kiss him full on the mouth. She smiled with great tenderness, her scent disturbing him but acting like a balm.

"We talked about it and you were certain that you wanted to be rid of Antonia," she said firmly. "Now you must write the other letters."

"Heath will be there soon and I have already ordered surveillance." She nodded and he looked into her face anxiously. "You promise to look after my son, Gerda?"

"It is convenient," she said. "I like to work and do not want to lose my body with children, so we shall be very happy."

"But later, we can have our children," he said, "If you want them."

She pulled up the back rest and put a pillow to make him comfortable. "That can wait. First I shall take you to Germany to meet my parents and I shall have everything a bride must have for the ceremony." Marcel swallowed hard. The idea of Gerda as a virgin bride was too much even for him.

Obediently, he pulled the small table closer, took out writing paper and began to write.

"Not overdoing it, I hope?" The camp doctor sat down in front of the fan and wiped the sweat from his sunburned face. "Christ! How much hotter will it be? I was frozen in Arkata, frozen and fried in Caillomo, depending on which side of the street I was standing, and now I can hardly breathe. How's the Soroche?"

"You think I may have altitude sickness?"

"Some." The doctor picked a handful of wet shirt and prised it from his chest. "Hell, Lambert, you don't know how lucky you are to have a fan." He evaded the dark enquiring eyes and wiped his arms on a towel hanging from a line between the tents. "Stay put for a while. Enjoy this while you can."

"Any results from the tests?"

"I'm growing a few cultures but it does show a gross infection apart from the crushing of tissue when that rock trapped you." He gave a false laugh. "Why worry. You are getting better, and with the lovely Gerda to nurse you, who could want to work?"

"Which means I am not fit to go back on site?"

"We'll get you walking this afternoon when it's cooler and see how you feel."

"What about sex?" Marcel hated asking that question but it was constantly on his mind.

"Gerda asked me that," the doctor said with a grin. "Seemed anxious, but I was pleased to tell her that you are not going to be limited in that area once the swelling has died down." He looked away. "I shall have to do more tests and, if necessary, when you go back home I advise a visit to a leading urologist to make sure that you have viable semen."

"You mean I may be sterile?"

"It's possible, but you are lucky. Didn't you say that your

wife is pregnant? One child is more than many people can manage, so be grateful." He saw the angry disbelief in Marcel's eyes. "It isn't certain by any means and only time and trial can tell us what is to be, but to be honest, it does look as if that rock gave you what amounts to a vasectomy."

"I don't believe it," Marcel said flatly.

"You did ask and I may well be wrong. We can't know until we do a few tests and I am not really equipped for that out here. Concentrate on your recovery and take it easy and who knows, you may be a father two or three times," the doctor added cheerfully.

"I was hoping to go to Kanacha," Marcel said sulkily. "I had no time to see the caves of Warari. I could go by helicopter the next time it comes to pick up and deliver."

"I know it isn't as bad as the Sierras but you can't risk that journey yet. Don't look so evil, Lambert. I know you have never been beaten by anything and you hate to feel that a bit of altitude sickness and a bad infection can hold you back, but you must remember that you also had a nasty attack of malaria, due, I suspect, to not taking the full dose of the prophylactic." He got up to go and stood in front of the fan for a minute.

"You left something on the table," Marcel pointed out. "You can't want more blood from me?"

"Er, no." The doctor looked embarrassed. "The helicopter will be here today and I wanted a specimen to send to the lab in Lima. Not blood, and not urine." He handed the container over to Marcel. "I think you might manage it now that the pain has gone and the sooner we know, the better." He grinned. "Just think of a luscious blonde and get turned on and the rest should be easy. I'll fix the tent zip and come back in ten minutes."

Marcel heard the zip close as if a more solid door closed forever. He was sweating again, but not from fever. He put his head in his hands for a minute, then shook himself. I must prove that I am whole, he thought, and when the doctor came back he lay exhausted and handed the glass jar to him without a word. He thought bitterly that he could have managed better with Gerda's help but she was nowhere in sight when the helicopter landed, shed its stores and took on board rock samples, the precious specimens and the home-going mail.

The doctor came back. "Cheer up," he said. "There are degrees. You may improve and in any case you could have artificial insemination for your wife if you want a big family." He looked sideways at the tense face, pale under the tan, and laughed. "You can still have your fun. Nothing wrong with the mechanism; just the shots. So you may be joining the blank-firing guns' club – many men pay good money to have it done."

"You bastard! You stinking bastard," Marcel whispered as he walked away.

Gerda came to him. "It is hot. I think a cool drink and some food?" She glanced at the letters that Marcel had completed. "All goes well, *ja*?" He caught at her hand but she turned away, taking the letters and running to the pilot of the helicopter. She came back breathless. "It is bad to run in this humidity. He brought very few letters," she added, giving Marcel the ones addressed to him.

"One from my lawyer," he said. "Antonia hasn't written. I must telephone my doctor to see that she is all right."

"Not now." Gerda's voice was sharp and Marcel felt his spirits lift. Gerda really did care for him enough to be jealous of his wife.

He laughed with his old vigour and kissed her on the mouth. "I have to check. She is the surrogate mother of our child, I am feeling better and you are the most beautiful woman in the world."

After supper, they sat with the others left at the base camp and watched the fireflies and the great unfamilar stars grow bright as night came. Soon he could make love again. Soon the others would leave him at the base camp with Gerda to look after him, and two students and a cook to make themselves useful. The helicopter would bring mail and supplies and he could relax.

He didn't believe the doctor and was happier than he had been for days. He went back to his tent, pleasantly tired, but stayed alone as he knew he couldn't beg Gerda to come to him. So much of pride was in the balance and he must be careful.

He slept and the chill of morning made him pull up a blanket. The radio was showing a red light and he picked up the headphone. "Geronimo!" a cheerful voice said. "We've made the link good again. Thought someone must be up by now." He spoke to someone and Marcel listened as the voice of a doctor from Lima came loud and clear.

"Message for your doc. Tell him that the guy with the sperm test is out of luck. Sorry, but it's definite, and permanent."

"Message understood, loud and clear. Out," Marcel said

mechanically. Thanks for nothing, he thought, but it was better to know. He thought of Antonia and sighed. He was no worse off. He wanted only one son and then a life with Gerda who wanted no children, so where was his problem?

Chapter Twelve

"Careful!" Robert held the canvas aloft and bent sideways to kiss the top of Antonia's head. She shut the door behind him and pulled aside the long velvet curtain that separated the tiny hall from the studio so that he could put the oil painting in a safe place. "Now you can attack me, woman," he said and held out his arms to her. She ran to the wonder of his strength and care, still fresh after what now seemed like forever and they stood close together in silence. Robert looked at her pale face. "What is it?" he asked.

"Two things. Both good, I think, but fairly shattering. Let's eat first and relax and then I'll tell you."

"I thought you had a class today. Not ill, are you?"

"Nothing bad," she insisted and went into the kitchen. "Soup and cold beef salad," she said. "I had no time to cook."

"I thought it was my turn. I wanted to finish that canvas but I expected to be galley slave tonight."

She turned away, shuddering slightly at the thought of the fish in the fridge waiting to be cooked. The idea of mackerel frying was repugnant. She took the wholemeal bread from the crock and sliced it, the fresh nutty smell making her hungry. "I lit the stove," she said.

"Cold? I hadn't noticed, but I suppose it does get chilly if we are up late and the wind rises. I ought to get more logs for the winter." He opened the door of the wood-burning stove and pushed in a piece of cherry wood. "We could use the rest of that tree. I might hire a chainsaw and take a day off to cut it up. It's going begging and Adrian said we might as well have it. We can heat the cottage for nothing more than my aching muscles."

The stripy cat which had appeared as if in answer to a newspaper advertisement as soon as Antonia moved into the cottage, took the best spot in front of the stove and went to sleep.

"I love wood fires," Antonia said. She put plates of meat on a low table and they sat on floor cushions in the glow escaping from the sides of the iron door. Robert examined the label on the wine bottle and looked at her quizzically. "I thought we'd spoil ourselves," she said, but he noticed that she drank very little and that most of the beef was on his plate. The warmth brought a glow to her face and her hands were no longer cold. Robert crunched an apple and watched her peel an orange. "I love this place," she said. "I want everything to stay exactly as it is now. This is my favourite time of the year."

"Then why so pale and sad when I came home?"

"Not sad." She move closer, her head on his lap and her hand caressing his knee. "You smell of turps and earth and love," she said.

"That's my life but not necessarily in that order." He thought back to the boy who had thrust away her love, clouded by the mistrust flung into his eyes by Marcel. He marvelled that she had ever forgiven him, and he had learned to be silent, to wait for her to confide, and to be there, aching with his need to give her his support, his love and his life. He smoothed her hair. "You've eaten nothing," he said.'

"I'm going to be very boring for a while," she said. "I had no idea I'd feel like this. We're going to have a child, Robert." She struggled to her feet and rushed for the bathroom. After ten minutes, she returned, pale and shaking. He wrapped her in a blanket and sat her on his knees in front of the fire. "I'm sorry," she said, smiling. "What a way to tell you! It suddenly struck me after you left this morning."

"You were asleep when I left but the alarm was set to get you up in time for your class."

"It went off and as soon as I raised my head I had to rush for the loo."

"I thought it only happened in the morning. Are you sure it isn't a tummy bug?"

"Quite sure. In fact I've had a few symptoms so I went over to the campus surgery to see John Campbell and have a test. He told me today that it's positive; as if I needed telling now!" she added. "He said that some women are sick at odd times so you'll have to get used to me and put up with it." She looked up at him and put out a hand to wipe the tear that began to run down his cheek. "Thank you for that," she said, softly.

They sat together for over an hour and her colour returned. "I'm ravenous now," she said.

201

"Do you want to eat coal or strange herbs?" he asked. "We can't afford out of season exotic fruits and caviare."

"I want bread and cheese and wine."

"Are you sure?"

He watched her tear a crust from the loaf and spread butter over it, adding pickle and cheese. "I warn you, I shall be a pain and quite unpredictable."

"I'll fit a door to the studio instead of the curtain. Does paint upset you?"

"I haven't been in there today," she said cautiously. "I think I'll do watercolour classes until this is better. I've only three more this session and we are both going to Edinburgh in two weeks' time, which will be pleasant and restful as I have only a couple of talks to give and no painty smells."

"Are you sure that you will be fit? You must say if there is anything you can't do. Nothing is more important than your health and happiness."

"I'll be very good." She stared out at the darkness and he got up to draw the curtains. "No, let them stay. I want to put out the light and see the trees. Did you notice how the chestnuts are turning? We ought to gather some blackberries before they are all gone."

"Mellow fruitfulness," he said. "You'll be a wonderful mother."

"I'm not the earth mother type but I shall love our child," she said. She moved closer to the window. "I heard from Marcel today."

"Oh, what now?" Robert felt wary. He had read the last letter that had been forwarded by Mrs Regan after being delayed in transit from South America, saying that he was shocked and disappointed by Antonia's attitude and that if divorce was what she wanted then he was the one who would have ample grounds to obtain one. "More riddles?"

She handed him a stiff envelope. "It's really from his lawyer. I can't understand it. How could he know that we are living together? I gave no hint to anyone who might write to him. He didn't know that I met you again and the most he can know is that I am teaching again against his wishes."

"Does it matter? It's evident that he intends accusing you of adultery even if he makes no mention of my name. Why worry? Technically, he's correct and I don't give a damn what is said if we can marry as soon as possible."

"This isn't like him. Do you think he was knocked on the head when the rocks fell? It's as if he wants a divorce as much as I do, yet when he went away it wasn't so. He made it clear that he wanted me as wife and mother, trapped forever because I had a baby." She glanced at the envelope. "I haven't really looked at the rest, beyond the beginning when he says that Marcel wants to sue for divorce on the grounds of adultery. I was far too busy being sick." She frowned. "It might have something to do with Gerda Baum. Maybe he finds he can't live without a big buxom blonde, instead of just having pictures in the bedroom. She'd suit him fine and be welcome to him."

"What the hell?"

"Robert?" She shrank back, half afraid of his fury. His red

hair flamed and the firm jaw jutted under the glossy beard. He tried to smile but the effort was too much. "Tell me?" she begged.

"The lawyer has been instructed to tell you that Marcel is suing for divorce, citing Randolph Heath as co-respondent, and saying that when your child is born he will claim complete custody as its father, stating that in view of your behaviour in his absence, you are no fit person to care for it."

"He can't! He has no baby. This is ours!"

"We know that, but he thinks that you were pregnant before he left home. He could try to say that it is his child."

"The dates are wrong."

"Not all that wrong," Robert said slowly. "What did John say? That you were several weeks pregnant? Marcel could insist that the baby was born late, and in law this baby was conceived while you were married to him. Many women have overdue births." His face was tense and he held her so tightly that she wanted to cry out. "He may try to take it but it will be over my dead body!"

"We must think," Antonia said, then dived for the bathroom as beads of sweat appeared on her forehead again. "I'm sorry," she said as soon as she returned shivering to the fire. Robert opened the iron door and a wave of hot air came from the exposed red hot fuel. "Why Randolph?" she asked. "I haven't seen the man for two years. I wasn't even there to say hello before I came here, and if I had it would have been under the eagle eye of Mrs Regan."

"This other letter slipped out of the envelope. It's a personal letter from the lawyer to you. It's fortunate that he knows you and has acted for both of you in the past."

"He's been a good friend," Antonia said. "He must feel badly about this." Robert handed her the letter and swished the screen-printed curtains across the window. They read the letter together.

Even couched in the oblique language of his profession, it became clear that Mr Ryan was puzzled. He referred to the orders he had received from Mrs Lambert, making him responsible for wages and other payments during her absence from the house until such time that she or Mr Lambert should return, and he assumed that she had lived elsewhere since the arrangements were made, on such and such a date. "Right so far, once we got through the gobbledegook," Robert said. "Just as well I have barristers in my family."

"Well, what more does he say?" Antonia asked.

"He goes on to say that he rang Mrs Regan to date the time of your leaving the house and she is sure that at no time have you returned, even for one night."

"Good old Paul Ryan," Antonia said. "He must be very embarrassed. He's been our joint legal adviser and acted for me about my mother's will and a property I once owned, so he can't know if he should act for me or for Marcel."

"There's more," Robert said. His face was stony as he handed her a small folder of photographs. "What's going on? How could he have got these? You were nowhere near the place."

Antonia left a thumbprint on the first snap and bent the edge as she tried to hold it still. It was a picture of her on the patio, wearing dark glasses. She knew when it was taken. "Remember when I said I was on the patio and saw a camera flash? I left my lunch on the table and went to fetch my sunglasses and then it happened. I thought it was a reporter."

The pictures were numbered in the order in which they were taken. Number two showed a woman in a loose-fitting dress walking up the drive, carrying a basket. The next was taken as she let herself in through the front entrance. In neither was the face visible. "*Did* you meet Randolph Heath?" Robert asked, in an agony of trying to be sane and fair. Two veins stood out on his brow, making a V sign like the tongue of a snake.

"You think I lied to you?" Antonia whispered.

"No! Never think that, but this makes my skin crawl. Others will believe it and he's obviously gone to a lot of trouble to frame you to make sure that he gets a divorce on his terms. We must get our facts straight so that we can fight him."

The next photograph was blurred as Mrs Regan saw him coming at her full face, and pushed the camera away, but the dress was the one that Antonia had given away before she left to join Robert, and the dark glasses were similar to her own. "I gave Mrs Regan a whole lot of my clothes and suggested that she got all the use out of them that she could before Marcel came back as he would object to her wearing my things." Robert stared at the next picture and then put a hand over his eyes.

Antonia picked it up and saw Randolph Heath reclining on a sunlounger on the patio. The fact that Mrs Regan was bending over him to catch a table napkin caught in a breeze did nothing to show that the couple were not laughing and touching one another. Once more, there was only an impression of dark hair and a pale profile of a woman but Randolph came out well, laughing and looking roguish.

"You can almost hear him laugh," Robert said. "They seem to be getting on really well!"

"He probably pinched her bum and she told him to give over," Antonia said in a dull voice. "Yes, here we are in the next one." His hand was flat on the woman's bottom and his eyes were speculative. "That horrible little punk must have spent hours getting those pictures," she said. "I never did like green Dyanne cars."

"He must have been very well paid."

"You mean that Marcel would do that?"

"Who else? You said he was on good terms with Gerda and she seems the type to get what she wants. He's set you up. He wants to compromise you with Heath, so he planted a man in the bushes to make sure he had evidence of you being together while the innocent husband was away working."

"But he could have a divorce without all that."

"You said that he was paranoic about having a child to resemble him and this is his way of making sure that he has custody."

"Does he hate me so much?" Her eyes sank into shadows of pain.

"He can't forgive you for loving me. Even though he knows that we never lived together before you married him he must know that he was living with only half a woman and resented every thought you gave to me." Robert gathered her into his arms. "He can't win this one, darling. I swear he can't."

"I must write to the lawyer to explain," Antonia said.

"Not tonight. Take a sleeping pill and get some rest. Did John give you any?"

"Mild sedatives and masses of vitamins. I'm so tired," she said.

He helped her to undress and put a hot bottle to her cold feet, tucking the clothes round her and a shawl over her feet. "That's wonderful," she said.

"Go to sleep. I'll slip in beside you later." He kissed her gently and went back to the sitting room, to read the rest of the letter that he had withheld from her. "He must be mad," he muttered. It was easy to see how Marcel's mind worked. Heath was an easy target as he had a bad reputation with women. The photographs were evidence enough in the eyes of a man blinded by arrogant possessiveness, even when he knew that Antonia was innocent.

Marcel had written a separate note. 'I have written to our own doctor asking him to make arrangements for you to enter a nursing home well before the time that you are to be delivered of my son or daughter. I insist that you have every possible care, and even if divorce proceedings are in progress, I want you to remain at our house until it is all over. I shall stay here for another month or so and then go to friends until we are legally free of our marriage.'

Antonia had assumed that all the contents of the big envelope were from the lawyer and had not seen Marcel's distinctive handwriting. What can I tell her? Robert thought. In her lowered state it wasn't fair to burden her with more than was necessary. In one way it was almost amusing. He could imagine the cold fury of the man when everything he had planned so carefully came to nothing, and if Gerda was looking forward to having a ready-made family with no risk to her own figure, then she would be disappointed.

The fact remained that one part of the letter had relevance. Antonia was pregnant. Robert shifted his weight on the floor cushion and poked at the open fire, sending the last of the sparks up to the grey maw of the chimney. That was true and Marcel might not want to be persuaded that the child wasn't his.

Robert sat for a long time, trying to think of ways to shield Antonia from any further trauma. Like many men faced with the miracle of reproduction for the first time on a personal level, he was vague about maternity. A woman got pregnant, grew steadily fatter and produced an infant in about nine months' time. That was the important bit: the timing. He went to the telephone and rang a number.

"John?" A mumble told him that perhaps half an hour after midnight wasn't the best time to ring a doctor unless it was urgent. "I'm sorry to ring so late. Antonia told me this evening."

"Christ, man! You haven't woken me up just so that I can congratulate you?"

"No, it's slightly more important than that. How pregnant is she?"

"Are you high? A woman is either pregnant or not. Antonia is preg. You can't be just a little bit preg!"

"I only want to know how far on she is."

209

"Why?" John's tone altered to one of cold suspicion. "You are living together, aren't you? Are you trying to say the baby isn't yours? As I see it, this is very much your responsibility. I've always liked Antonia, Robert, and I won't have her messed about by you or anyone. You've been living together for long enough to make this possible, and I can't think that she would sleep around. That isn't Antonia."

"Cool it! It's only because I am so concerned that I had to get in touch this late. It's very important. How many weeks or months? Can you tell? What if someone said she was four or five months pregnant? Would you be able to say it wasn't so?"

"Certainly not four months. I can't as yet feel anything externally. If she was four months I would be able to palpate the uterus over the symphyses, or to put it plainly to an ignoramus like you, I'd feel a lump behind the bone over her pussy." He yawned. "Now unless you want the full history of pregnancy, can I get back to sleep?"

"So it's a matter of weeks and not months?"

"Several weeks, which just about fits in with the time she's been at the cottage with you. Tell her to come and see me next week and to keep on taking the tablets."

Robert undressed and tried to get into bed without disturbing Antonia but her hand wandered over to him in her sleep and he pressed it tenderly. He was going to be a father. Nothing like this emotion had ever filled him with such protective love for the woman at his side. He was conscious of rising fury towards the man who had kept her from her rightful mate and now wanted to rob her of her child.

Sleepless, he thought of Marcel and how he would be when he knew that his obsession would give him nothing. I wish that Antonia had told him as soon as she left the house, he thought. If it was me, I'd be desperate, he admitted to himself. John must write to the lawyer stating his diagnosis, thus letting him get in touch with Marcel with the facts. He blessed the instinct that had made him so sure that Antonia must come to him before Randolph Heath arrived. There had been no contact, not even a handshake in greeting, so Marcel couldn't accuse Antonia of misconduct with her guest, and the fact that she couldn't be more than six weeks pregnant must convince any judge that the child she carried could not be her husband's.

Robert tried to sleep but had to get up to fix the creaking window-frame. He looked out at the scene they both loved and knew that he must fight for their future.

It was cold before dawn and he brought in an extra blanket to throw over the sleeping woman. He made tea and sat by the embers, too weary to make up the fire and yet not ready for sleep. At eight, he woke to hear Antonia vomiting in the bathroom and he heaved himself from the cushions, cursing his cramped legs.

When Antonia came in, the fire was lit over the still-warm ashes and the kettle boiling ready for tea. "Thanks," she said gratefully, huddling against the warm stove. "I get so cold when I'm sick."

"It will be better very soon," Robert said.

"Oh, what do you know about it?" she asked and smiled.

"I learn fast," he said, handing her a mug of tea with the air of a conjuror producing a miracle from a hat.

"You'll have to start all over again, I'm afraid," she said. "This tea tastes terrible."

He sipped his own and looked puzzled.

"It's me, not the tea," she realised. "John did mention that I might go off a few things and tea was one of them."

"Coffee?"

"Bovril, I think. Do we have any?" She went to the kitchen and came back with a meat stockcube crumbled in boiling water. "Delicious," she said.

"But you don't like that!"

"I do now. I also feel that I need something to eat but I can't make up my mind what it is I do want."

"Oh, God! You of all people! I never thought I'd see the day when you'd be fussy over food."

"I shall buy lots of oranges and some sardines and wholemeal bread. Shall I start making my own bread? It's creative and healthy and I think I'm going to eat a lot of it."

"Sounds a good idea, but for the next few days while you are throwing up you must rest."

"For how long?"

"I'm not sure."

"Didn't John say?" She smiled, with some of her normal humour. "I was too sleepy to listen closely, but it sounded like an antenatal clinic in there last night."

"I had to know that everything was all right," he said, sheepishly.

"Bless you." She snuggled into the crook of his arm.

"Steady! The last time I kissed you, you ran off to be sick. It's a bit demeaning to have that effect on the woman you love."

"Not this time. I shall work well today. I know it. Why do I feel so happy?"

He kissed her. "Stay happy," he said.

"I can read the rest of that stuff now," she said.

"Later."

"No, I want to read it now and get it over."

"Feeling strong?"

"Do I need to be?" Her face paled.

"It's nothing that you don't know, or almost all." He hugged her close but she struggled away. "Marcel wants you to go into a nursing home of his choice when the birth is imminent, and after the baby is born. Before then, he insists that you have every care in his house until the divorce is final." She stared at him, trying to think clearly. "Just try to think of this from his angle for a minute. He thinks that you are living at the house now. He doesn't know that you left before Heath took up residence and he doesn't know about us. As far as Marcel is concerned, he has a wife who is pregnant, made so by him four months ago, living at home with the man he now cites in the divorce plea and he thinks that it gives him a lever to make the courts give him custody of the baby."

"But this baby is not his!"

"I know that, you know it and John Campbell, our own doctor knows it. Poor Randolph Heath must wonder what's hit him if

213

he has been told that he's been a very naughty boy and hasn't even had the fun of it!"

"What can I do, Robert?"

"Not what *you* can do, my love. This is you and me and our baby together. If you'd taken when we made love in France, then we might have been in a very difficult situation, as a pregnancy conceived then could easily be confused with one started a week or so earlier."

She nodded. "He forced me to have sex several times during our last three days together." She saw the pain in Robert's eyes and went on gently. "Even if I had never met you again, I had decided that my marriage was over and that I could never live with him again."

She watched him pull at his beard and knew that he was very worried. "He's not going to believe us," Robert said, flatly. "Whatever we say he will brush aside as lies and swear that the child was conceived in wedlock. We must be prepared to face a lot of hassle until we can prove that the baby is ours."

"I'd rather lose it than let him touch it." Antonia said slowly, with such cold passion that Robert shuddered. "I'd rather have an abortion and wait for our family until after the divorce, and he can have a whole tribe of blond giants by Gerda Baum."

"You can't. I want this baby as much as you do. If there is one child born of love, then this is it, and it will be ours." He stroked her hair and waited until her pulse was normal. "He's not due back yet and when he does return he isn't going to live at the house until after the divorce, which he obviously thinks will be a quickie." He gave a short laugh. "Can't you imagine it? The wronged husband refusing to cross the doorstep of the house where he has been betrayed but ready to give his wife every support until she is delivered? It will also scotch any attempt to say that if he did return and stayed in the same house as you, what was to stop him having sex with you and so making the divorce plea a farce?"

"Why does he bother? Divorce is easy and we could have agreed about it and stayed apart."

"If he wants the child he has to make you seem immoral and so incapable of being a good mother."

"Is it all worth it?" she cried. "I don't think I can face it. Wouldn't it be better if I saw John . . . ?" She burst into tears and he hushed her gently.

"During the next few weeks, there will be many times when you feel low and are convinced that nothing can come right." He made her look at him. "Promise me that you will do nothing silly to harm either yourself or our baby."

"I promise," she said, but her emptiness was not wholly due to lack of food. "When do I get over this sicky-weepy stage?"

"Have another chat with John," he suggested. "That is, if he's still talking to me! He's already written me off as just another hysterical father."

"You?" The colour flowed back into her cheeks. "I had no idea you could be like this. It's wonderful. I promise to do everything that I'm told and take great care of my health."

"The rest will follow. No way can Marcel take our child. Let him start his own dynasty of French-German stock. That woman looks as if she could have a litter!"

"He wanted a son to look like him, and I am dark like him," Antonia said. She shrugged. "Maybe if he really loves her he will want them all blonde and beautiful like Gerda, and be glad to see the back of me." She cleared away the dishes and Robert raked out the dead ashes to make the fire up anew.

Chapter Thirteen

"At least you are over the worst," said Dr John Campbell.

"I wouldn't dare to do anything that my bullying doctor said was forbidden," Antonia said, smiling. She sipped her white wine. "And don't peer into my glass to see what I'm drinking! This is a celebration and I shall have no more than one glass of wine and perhaps a small glass of dry sherry later. Surely that isn't excessive?"

"Whatever you are doing, it suits you. I've seldom seen a more blooming specimen."

"You are so flattering, John! You make me feel like a test-tube being held up to the light for inspection."

"Well, I have to talk like that. It's hardly the time to tell you I fancy you, is it?" he said dryly. "Have you considered where you might have the baby?"

"As close to Robert as I can. You say it's due in late March, early April or thereabouts, so Robert should be here teaching at that time. The local cottage hospital looks good from what I've seen of it in outpatients and the relaxation classes."

"I've already made a provisional booking there and I assure you that they are very efficient." He picked the cherry from his glass and ate it. The rest of the party were at the other end of the huge room that served Adrian as a sitting room and, when required, as an official interview room. It was perfect for parties.

Antonia glanced at the group of senior students who were laughing and teasing Robert. She smiled. His new role of caring companion and prospective father had calmed the raw passion and mellowed him in his dealings both with her and his students and colleagues.

Adrian had such good ideas, she decided. After Christmas was always a dull time, and the students were restless and unwilling to concentrate when the world outside was grey and cold. The party that he held as soon as the students returned from the Christmas break seemed to set the pace for the term and made a good atmosphere for work and social contacts.

"You haven't given any thought to the other plan?" John asked.

She looked at him, forgetting what they had been discussing. "Other plan?"

"The nursing home near your old house." John led her to a seat by a radiator. "I wanted to have a chat when Robert was out of the way. I'm usually busy when he's teaching and when he's free he hardly leaves your side and I can't find you alone."

"Not trying to chat me up, are you?" she asked with the easy affection that came with mutual respect and trust.

"Too late for both of us," he said with a grin. "Seriously,

Antonia, I ought to say a few things. Bruce Marden wrote to me when I asked for your medical records, and he told me of your husband's wishes."

"Bruce should learn to mind his own business," she said.

"He still looks on you as his patient and will do until you officially request a change of doctor. Get that form off tomorrow."

"I've already done that. He should have it by now."

"In some ways he is right," John said. "Legally you are married to Marcel Lambert and your address as his wife is the one you left when Marcel was away in South America."

"*Was* in South America? He is still there."

"No, he came back last week and was staying with friends."

"How do you know?"

"Antonia, I don't know your husband, but from the few phone calls we had after exchanging letters, Bruce Marden gave me a very serious picture of him." John was no longer smiling. "I need another drink. Don't go away, there's more."

With growing unease, she watched him walk back with a fresh drink in his hand. He was making an effort to appear unconcerned, which did nothing to reassure her. She waited impatiently while he sampled his whiskey. "Tell me," she begged.

"Bruce thinks you may have trouble and wanted to know your plans."

"So that he can tell Marcel?"

"I'm not sure. What he did say was that Marcel came to him in a blazing temper, acccusing him of aiding and abetting you in a fraud. He refuses to believe that the child you are carrying is not his and swears that you went away so that Bruce couldn't examine you and give Marcel the information he needed. Bruce had to admit that he had never examined you, as you said that you were not pregnant because your period had started after Marcel left."

"That is true."

"He has only your word for that, and sometimes, not often but it does happen, a little loss can happen during the first month." He sighed. "He seems to have spent the last week accusing everyone he meets of some misdemeanour, from your housekeeper to your lawyer."

"Just as well that Randolph left before Christmas," Antonia said. "Mrs Regan told me in her Christmas card."

"Your husband refuses to let him off the hook. He swears that you must have stayed in that house with Heath and now you have moved on to another lover. Better and better for him if that was true, but it didn't improve his temper when he found out with whom you are now living."

"You seem to know a lot about it all."

"More than you think. Remember that as a doctor I can ask questions that refer to your condition and get answers. I had to know the cause of your earlier depression and when I asked Robert, he was glad to confide in someone. Together with my professional contact with Dr Bruce Marden, I probably know most of what is going on and can keep you briefed about your husband."

"You *are* on my side, John?"

"Of course I am! No. Forget that, as we are talking seriously. This is purely a matter between doctor and patient. I have to act in your best interests and tell the truth about your condition if it is necessary to discuss it." He looked sternly Scottish. "In law, your husband has the right to know the truth so if I pass on information about your health, but only about your health, Bruce Marden has the right to pass it on to Marcel." He looked into her eyes. "I shall stick to the truth and refuse to discuss your way of life apart from the pregnancy. In no way can this be the child of Marcel Lambert and I'll fight anyone who tries to prove otherwise. As soon as the baby is born I shall take blood for tests to prove paternity, just as another safeguard."

"But you aren't happy about it? John, you are holding something back."

"Happy enough about my own convictions and the facts, but the child will be born in wedlock and the divorce isn't final until afterwards. You may have a fight on your hands. I think you ought to stay here even if pressure is brought to persuade you to go into the nursing home suggested by your husband. My advice as a doctor is to go into hospital early for a check, before you are in labour, as your blood pressure is up slightly. No, don't look worried. It might just be stress and is a matter of little concern if it stays at this level, but I can truthfully say that I want to keep a careful watch on you and I shall write to Bruce Marden saying just that, before it returns to normal!"

"Bless you," she said. "Do you know where Marcel is now?"

"He went to Germany as soon as he had thoroughly upset everyone. He had a colleague with him when Bruce saw him."

"A woman? Blonde and statuesque?"

"How did you quess?"

"She appeared on TV with him and I gather that he has plans for her when the divorce is through."

"Can't they beget their own? She sounds fit enough."

"By now, it doesn't matter to Marcel that this child may not be his. What matters to him is that a plan he made shows signs of failing and he'd hate me to get away from him without the maximum of suffering." She shivered. "I hope he stays in Germany."

"He'll be back soon. If he still believes that you were pregnant before he went away, he must think that results will appear in February. It could be at any time then, give or take a week or so. If you have to see your lawyer, as you mentioned, make it next week at the latest while he's away and get back here ready to raise the drawbridge and put down the portcullis. We'll keep you safe." It was said lightly but Antonia squeezed his hand gratefully. "Take care, me dear," he added and raised his glass to her in solemn salute before turning away to the door.

Robert came over. "Going so soon?" he asked, taking his place by Antonia's side.

"I do have other patients. I can't stay here watching one wine-swilling primagravida. See you both, and remind me to take you to see the maternity staff a bit nearer the time. You ought to get to know them, Antonia. It's a pity they don't use the same staff in the relaxation classes, but the physio girls like to do that here. We'll fix a meeting soon. Robert ought to show his face there too."

"Tired?" Robert asked.

"Not really. Just a nice weary feeling after my exercises this afternoon."

She held his hand as they walked back to the cottage and heard the wind through the leafless trees. It was true, and she tried to push away the thoughts that John had stirred up.

"You've never painted the poplars after leaf fall," he said. "Next year, you should try it. I like stark branches against a winter sky. There's a nice filigree of twigs up there."

"Next year, when it's all over and we are married. Next year when we have our baby, I shall think about it, but now, I'm broody and I want my warm nest and security and nothing but my home, and you and the baby."

"Hey there! I thought we were over the blues."

"Yes, it's just that I'm content the way things are and in winter the trees look more like the ones in the Hobbema in Holland. Famous it may be, but I always think that the Avenue de Middel Harnos looks like an avenue of poplars with the bottom branches shaved away. I prefer ours, and when the spring comes I shall paint them in first tiny leaf."

The telephone was ringing and Robert left her abruptly. He opened the door and went in to answer it, then handed the receiver to her. "For you," he said. "A bit late even for telephone selling. A woman," he added. He shrugged and went to put the kettle on.

"Hello," Antonia said.

"That is Mrs Marcel Lambert?"

"I am Antonia Lambert," she said.

"Oh, I'm so glad I managed to contact you. My name is Miss Bentinck and I'm the matron of the Hollowdene Private Hospital. I understand that you will be coming to us soon and I'm rather concerned that we have never met or had any personal interview."

"There must be some mistake, Miss Bentinck. I have no booking with you."

"I don't understand. Your husband was very explicit. He told me that you had been away for a few months but now that he was back from his expedition you would be returning home and coming to us to have your baby."

"How did you find me?"

"Your housekeeper gave me a forwarding address but I found that it was only a professional contact at the university so I asked your own doctor and he gave me this number and your real address. You are a very long way from home, Mrs Lambert." The voice was full of reproach. "How can we give you the attention you need from that distance, especially as your husband had to go away to Germany on urgent business? I really think you should come down here and see me before you go into labour. What will your husband think if you run any risks just now?" She sighed. "Someone must be responsible for you."

Antonia could almost see her face. The woman would have pursed lips. Like a hen's bottom, Granny would have said. The self-righteousness told its own tale of Marcel hinting that his wife was difficult and eccentric and very sloppy in her arrangements.

"It really is too bad of my husband." Antonia's voice oozed

reason and sympathy as she replied. "I'm afraid that there has been a mistake. I hate putting anyone to such inconvenience, but that is just what my husband has done. I am living here permanently now. I shall have my baby in the local hospital when the time comes. I am having relaxation classes and frequent examinations from the university doctor and when the time comes I have only a hundred yards to walk to the maternity block. Rest assured, I am having every care. My doctor thinks that the baby isn't due yet so I don't need to be admitted."

"I don't understand." Obviously she thinks I'm mad and telling a pack of lies, Antonia thought. "Mr Lambert was so positive and he didn't strike me as being a man who didn't know his own mind."

"I do know when my own baby is due," Antonia said. "I have to see my lawyer this week. I shall be in the area for just one afternoon. Would it help if I came to see you to convince you that I am not near the time for delivery?"

"Yes. Yes, that would help. Can you make it soon?" Miss Bentinck said, as if Antonia might drop the baby on the carpet.

Antonia looked at Robert, who stood ready with Bovril and toast. "Shall we say tomorrow at four o'clock, just before I come back home?"

"That would suit me very well. Shall I alert your doctor?"

"That isn't necessary. I may drop in to see him earlier," she lied. "It will have to be a quick visit and I haven't time after my appointment with the lawyer to stay late, as I hate driving in too much traffic."

"What was all that about?" Robert asked.

She told him the gist of the conversation. "I might as well convince yet another person that Marcel is mad," she said.

"I can't let you go there alone."

"We both know that I have to make at least one trip there. I have no intention of visiting the house and this can be fitted in very well. Marcel is away and in a way I want to go alone."

In bed, she wriggled closer and her lips brushed his cheek. "I feel fine," she said. "John says it's all right even though I did seem to have more than my fair share of morning sickness. Only an accident, a shock, or something he objects to having for breakfast can damage the baby now."

He stroked her hair and caressed her full breasts, following the blue lines of the now prominent veins in the whiteness. He took her gently and she was passive, wondering at the depth of their love, without the passion of their first lovemaking. She lay relaxed. "I'm glad we could be together again tonight before you go there," he said. She took his hand and laid it on the risen mound and he pressed gently and then stopped, his hand frozen over the tiny convulsion under the muscle. "Quickening is still the best name for this," he said. "Hello, first born, or about to be."

Robert lay awake for a long time after Antonia was breathing deeply, but was sound asleep when she appeared with tea. "I want to be away early," she said. "I'll have lunch somewhere before I see the man."

Robert looked at the sky as he opened the car door. "Warm

enough? It seems milder and there is no bad weather forecast so you should have a good trip."

A dimple appeared in her cheek. "Thank you for having me, sir," she said.

The fallen leaves were dark with winter rain and a copper-coloured spaniel ran through the sodden remains, his coat the colour of the leaves. For no reason it made her want to cry, but as soon as she reached the motorway, she was calmly planning the day ahead. This was another milestone. Once she had signed the papers that the lawyer held for her about the sale of the last of her unwanted furniture and some trinkets that would be more useful as cash, and once the mix-up about the maternity booking was sorted out, she could turn her back on the past and concentrate on having a baby.

Bruce wouldn't be pleased when he found out that she had been in town without seeing him, but she felt that the less he knew about her affairs the better, as Marcel had been his friend for years. Once more, she blessed the fact that she had a little income of her own and had taken nothing from the account left for her by Marcel when he went away. I'm even independent of Robert, she thought. Not that it mattered, but it was a good feeling to be free, to be with him but to have enough money to pay her way.

She enjoyed the drive and soon recognised familiar landmarks. She slowed down, unwilling to let the old life impinge yet on her new security. She lunched away from the main road, choosing a coffee shop that sold hot food and was unlikely to be used by anyone she knew. Eating now was no problem and her appetite was almost too good. She resisted the urge to eat a second roll with her soup and settled for a large salad instead of the fragrant lasagne that was the dish of the day.

In the restroom she caught sight of herself, side view, and smoothed down her full skirt. There was a slight overall plumpness as well as the thickening of her waist, but not too bad, she decided, and remembered an old loose coat she had kept that would be warmer and would button over her lump more comfortably.

She parked in the supermarket car park and walked down the high street to the office. The building was tucked away between the launderette and a hamburger bar. How would old Mr Ryan have regarded that? When he ruled the firm of Ryan, Dupont and Ryan, the building had been separated from its neighbours by an elegant shrubbery enclosed by wrought-iron, but simple economics and the demand for space in the growing town made it sensible to sell and bring the elbows of the narrow house closer.

"Ah, yes, Mrs Lambert. Mr Ryan is expecting you. Please go straight in." Antonia held in her stomach as much as she could, aware that the secretary was watching her as she walked to the office door, but the loose skirt and top hid a lot. Sorry to disappoint you, dear, Antonia thought, and knew that there must have been speculation among the staff about her date of delivery.

"Mrs Lambert, this is a pleasure." She was offered a comfortable chair and coffee arrived as if by magic. "First let us go through your private papers," Mr Ryan said. "I have all the necessary documents ready." Antonia checked the neatly set out will and testament that she had asked him to prepare. "Very wise. I wish that more young people would settle these matters; it saves such a lot of heartache in many cases. Now you can forget about it, unless you change your mind, or circumstances change for you or you live to be a hundred and have spent it all!"

"It's a relief," she said, and sighed. Now nothing of hers could ever be administered by Marcel. They agreed on the rest of her investments from the sale of the last few pieces of old jewellery and Mr Ryan poured more coffee, looking slightly uneasy. "Now we come to the other matter," he said, and coughed.

"The divorce," Antonia said calmly. "As far as I am concerned, it can't be over quickly enough." She smiled to reassure him.

"Your husband came in here in what I can only describe as a very aggressive mood. He insists that you are carrying his child and demands complete custody of the infant immediately after the birth. The divorce is going through quickly as he applied for it before he left for South America on quite simple grounds, plus the accusation that you committed adultery with an unnamed man."

"Before he left? You mean he planned to compromise me with just anyone who turned up and was available?" Antonia laughed.

"I am in a difficult position in that I act for both of you in various ways. It does happen, of course, but there are certain aspects of this case that are . . . unusual, to say the least."

"I do sympathise. As far as I am concerned he can divorce me on whatever grounds he can find that are true so long as

229

he doesn't cite Randolph Heath, who I have not seen for at least two years. Under no circumstances am I going to contact Marcel again unless I am forced to do so. I am booked in at the local hospital close to the university where I work and live now, and the doctor there is very attentive. By now, Marcel knows that I am living with Robert Blackberne, a man I knew before I met Marcel, and the baby I am carrying is Robert's. Surely Marcel can't want the child of another man?"

"That's where he is being very difficult, and to be honest, just between these walls, I think he's a trifle unhinged." Mr Ryan looked very unhappy and drank more coffee. "He wants *your* child; he is convinced that the joining together of your genes and his will result in a child exactly like him, dark-haired, brown-eyed, intelligent and artistic."

"That's sick! He can sire nurseries full of children by another woman. Pay for one with the right colouring to act as surrogate to his semen if that will turn out what he wants, but this child will not be like him. It will be like Robert, so Marcel must either settle for Gerda's offspring or choose another dark-haired mate."

"It isn't that simple."

"Why not?"

"You heard that he was injured when they had that rock fall?"

"Of course, but I can't see what that has to do with this matter."

"He was injured and after that had an infection. Together this rendered him infertile, at least for a time, and probably for good, as irreversible as a badly done vasectomy that turned septic."

"I don't believe it." Her head began to spin and Mr Ryan looked anxious. "I'm fine," she said and sat straighter. "Really fine, thank you."

"If he can have this child, it will prove to him that his manhood was not in question and the accident could have happened to anyone." He looked solemn. "He obviously chose you quite deliberately to fulfill certain functions and thought of you as the best choice as the mother of his child."

"The dates are wrong," Antonia said. "My doctor will swear that I could not have been pregnant before Marcel left the country. This baby belongs to Robert Blackberne!" The lawyer winced. "Is it necessary to mention names?"

"Mention his name? I shall shout it from the housetops for everyone to hear if it will convince the world that the child is his. It can't hurt us and it might make Marcel think again. When he comes back, will you make it plain to him that I have gone forever, I am never coming back and I am expecting the child of another man; the man I should have married but who was deceived about me by Marcel Lambert." Mr Ryan seemed about to protest but she waved this aside.

"I also want him to know that if he doesn't leave us alone, I shall sue him for defamation or something. Surely he can't just plan my divorce and disgrace on grounds supplied by false witnesses? Have you seen the photographs of Mrs Regan and Randolph Heath?"

"I have seen them and have obtained affidavits from both parties that you are not involved, but your husband chooses to ignore my statements and continues to have this *idée fixe* about you." He dropped his dry style of speech. "If I were you, I'd have the baby quietly and then get away, far enough for him to lose touch, and keep away for a few months. I can see to anything you want me to do here and I promise not to divulge your whereabouts."

"Thank you. I have the same thoughts. I think I know where I shall go."

"Write to me at the time and mark it personal and confidential, but don't tell me now," he said. "The less I know now, the better." His parting handshake was warm and Antonia sensed that he was genuinely concerned for her welfare. The girl in the outer office smiled and gave her a neat folder for her papers and Antonia went to find the car.

The private hospital was in a pleasant part of the town similar to the area where her old home had been, but Antonia was relieved to find that she had no need to cover old ground, and her route home could be reached from that side of the town as soon as she finished with the matron.

She sat in the plush waiting room for five minutes before the matron swanned in, all crispness, pursed lips as Antonia had imagined and a rather incongruous wave of Joy perfume.

It took a little while for Antonia to establish the fact that she was telling the truth about her condition, and in any other circumstances it would have been amusing to see the incredulous slackening of the self-righteous lips to puzzlement and confusion.

"Have you heard from Dr Marden today?" Antonia asked casually.

Matron blushed. "Yes, he told me that he had received your change of doctor form and was no longer in charge."

"So you did get in touch with him after I telephoned? I suppose you reported to Mr Lambert too?"

"I thought it advisable. How was I to know . . . ? Your husband appears to be away so I didn't speak to him, but I shall have to write and say that it is obvious that you will not be coming to us next week."

"Not next week or any week," Antonia said firmly. "I'm sorry that he put you in this embarrassing situation, Matron. If I could advise you?" The woman nodded. "Don't contact him directly. Send your letter to the solicitor and let him deal with any further letters, and be sure to charge him for the cancelled booking. I'm sure that you deserve compensation." She turned at the door. "Goodbye. I'm glad that you know that I, at least, am not the one who is completely mad."

"And goodbye to this town and everything in it," she said thankfully as she drove home to Robert and the cottage and contentment. Marcel was now so thoroughly unpopular that he would find it hard to gain allies in spite of all his devious methods and lies. *I'm safe from him for all time,* she thought and felt the child stir more vigorously than ever. She laughed softly. Everything would be fine, and the headache that had started in the private hospital must be psychological, surfacing at the mention of Marcel's name, but it niggled all the way home.

Chapter Fourteen

"I suppose a young baby is all right travelling by plane?" said Robert. "It's not very far to France but a bit of an ordeal for an infant, surely?" he looked anxious. "I've booked our auberge in Normandy and had no trouble there as they have no other person interested at the moment. We can be flexible about times, depending on the date of birth and if we have to go there early, Madame can give us two rooms. She sounded delighted to hear our news."

"How are they? You seemed to be a long time on the phone."

"She wanted to tell me all the news. Guess what? Jacqueline is going to marry the student who was there when we were staying there."

"He'll be sorry that he taught her all those swear words and obscenities." She laughed.

"Do babies get seasick or airsick? We could go by sea but if the wind is high and it's rough on the water, that might be worse than going by air."

"Stop fussing, Robert. The baby isn't due yet. You keep hovering round me as if I am about to lay an egg." Antonia shifted her bulky body to a more or less comfortable position. "I wish it was over. I feel as big as a bus and just as clumsy." Her normally trim ankles were swollen and it was an effort to walk across from the cottage to the main block to see John Campbell, but she knew that he was expecting her in half an hour. "I'll help you pack when I come back, but I must go to see John," she said.

"I think I'll stay. They can manage without me for the first two days. On Sunday, I could drive up with you and I could keep an eye on you, that is if John thinks you should travel just now."

"No, you must go, Robert. I don't feel like travelling and I can eat in the cafeteria and not do much here while you forget about all this and take your lectures. If you do this extra work now, we can have more time free later. What a clever baby to be born when the department is slack." She put out a hand so that he could pull her up from the chair. "Oh, where is the lissom girl you once loved?"

"In there somewhere, and I still love her." He watched her walk away slowly and then tried to concentrate on the contents of his briefcase. He had all the papers he needed for the seminar and knew that the work he had sent in advance had been received with enthusiasm but he was uneasy. If only this had been a couple of weeks ago, he thought, when Antonia was sparkling; now, the slightest exertion made her feel limp and she had put on a lot of weight. The baby was due in three or four weeks, John said, but he couldn't be more certain than that.

Robert snapped the case shut. Even if she is delivered in two weeks' time, I have plenty of time to give my lectures and be back here with days to spare, he decided. Adrian and his wife had promised to look in every day to see Antonia and John was on call and very near. The telephone was by the bed and he knew that his own anxiety was getting to her and making her nervous.

An hour passed and Antonia was still away. Robert finished packing and loaded up Antonia's car, which he was now using as she could no longer drive in comfort. He heard her footsteps, heavy on the concrete. "Do I go or stay?" he asked. "What did John say?"

"You go. Sorry I'm late back but he was busy. Everything fixed? Did you pack enough shirts?"

"Plenty for six days. I'll ring every day and if I have bad vibes about you I'll come back early."

She touched his cheek. "Be good and come back soon. I need you there when the baby is born."

"I'll be there, even if I did chicken out of the classes and the cosy get-together with the staff. I wouldn't go into a labour room with just any woman, but for you, my love, I'd have the baby myself. I hope I don't pass out," he added, as if that possibility had only now presented itself.

"If only you could have it," she said with feeling. "I'm a bit tired of it. Nine months is a very long time. Couldn't you do the next bit?"

She watched the car until it vanished beneath the overhanging hedge at the end of the driveway, then wandered back under the sighing branches that held a promise of leaf. Spring and sap are rising but this year I shall feel nothing, she thought. I'm heavy and awkward and not very happy.

She sat by the window and looked out. John would be furious when he knew that Robert had gone. Her blood pressure was up, there was more fluid in the tissues than he liked to see and her weight was all wrong, but she couldn't bear to watch Robert suffering. The telephone rang. "No, John, I didn't tell him. He's well on the way now." She listened while he yelled at her and then put down the phone. I'll go to bed now, she decided. Pity about the fluids being restricted. It would be nice to have a long cool drink just now, but John had been firm about the amount she was allowed in each twenty-four hours.

The telephone rang again. "Mrs Lambert? This is Miss Granger, the sister in charge of maternity. Dr Campbell wants you in for checks. Is it all right if I send a car for you or do you need an ambulance?"

"Now? I saw Dr Campbell an hour ago and he didn't mention it."

"He had your specimen tested and wants more tests done in here. Nothing to worry you, but we do need to keep a graph about what's going on and maybe put the baby on a monitor." Her voice was light and young but very firm.

"Yes, Sister."

"Pack a few things in case we keep you overnight."

"I'll be ready in half an hour." It was a relief to have someone who knew what she was talking about take over and make all the decisions. Antonia filled a bag with toilet things, a nightdress and tissues. None of her dressing gowns fitted any more so she took a voluminous affair that Robert wore on the beach and the car arrived as soon as she was ready. The driver took her case when they arrived at the side door of the unit.

Antonia looked about her. "I've never seen this department," she said and recalled that John had suggested that she and Robert must introduce themselves to the maternity staff, but they had put it off. She had gone to the classes and to see John regularly and had thought that they had plenty of time to meet the others.

"A pity your husband is away," Sister Granger said with a hint of reproof. "I like to meet all prospective fathers so that they can share the whole experience." She gave an unexpected smile. "I'm all for them sharing the good and the bad. Makes them more caring if they see what you have to do. Is he going to be here when you are in labour?"

"Yes. Dr Campbell suggested it and Robert was anxious to be with me. He had to go away for a few days but he should be back long before the baby is due."

"You have his phone number?"

"I have several. One for the hotel and one for the conference centre and another for the secretary who will know exactly where he is lecturing from day to day. A message can get to him easily and he will ring me every day. I'll ring him later if I have to stay overnight."

She was aware of her own heartbeat, loud and heavy and

beating in her ears as the sister took a fresh reading of her blood pressure. "Is everything all right?" she asked. "The baby seems to be pressing down further today. Can I go to the loo? I seem to have frequency again. The baby must be much lower."

"Put a specimen in this jar. I know you had one done earlier but we might need another and I shall need to take some blood."

When Antonia came back, carrying a very cloudy offering in the specimen jar, the sister had a syringe ready to take blood. "We'll do this now to save time later. We do a few tests as routine and they give us a clear picture of your condition. We also need your blood group and a sample for cross-matching if you need to be given any extra blood."

"Why would I need that?"

"Some women are anaemic," Sister said in a soothing voice and Antonia closed her eyes as she saw the blood flow sluggishly into the syringe. She felt sick. There would be blood when the baby came and she and Robert shared a dislike of all things surgical. Poor darling, he did want to do what was right, but he would hate it. She smiled and the nausea faded.

"Any backache? Any discomfort?" The bright eyes were watchful, seeing everything. "You'd be much more comfortable lying down. That's right. Off with those shoes and I'll send Nurse to get you undressed."

"Am I staying here? I ought to ring Adrian to feed my cat."

"Have you his number?" Antonia pointed to her purse. "Who is Adrian?"

"He's the head of the art faculty. His wife feeds my cat if

we are away and we do the same for theirs. Adrian Corder." The ceiling was fuzzy and it was too much trouble to look up numbers. "Help yourself, Sister, and thank you. It's the little black book. I am quite good at noting telephone numbers. They are all there." It was wonderful to sink back onto soft pillows.

Undressed and cool, Antonia tasted a sedative on her tongue and the headache had stopped. She was no longer aware of backache or the strange twinges that flitted over her abdomen since the injection that Sister said was routine.

"Absolute rest," she heard and sensed that John came to see her, but she was too weary to sit up and be sociable. She knew that he would understand. She was thirsty, but they only cooled her lips with something wet and put a cold bag on her head to take away the ache. I haven't had a real headache for ages, she thought. Marcel used to bring one on as soon as I saw him or when he looked at me with disapproval. He was gone, thank God. With luck she would never have to see him again.

"A bed pan?" Antonia giggled. "I never thought I'd have to have a bed pan but I suppose everyone does here."

"Everyone does," the smooth voice agreed. Such strong arms and I must weigh a ton, she thought. Such nice clean smells and such safety.

The night went in dreams that eddied round in her head with Sam from the hotel in France saying that he liked all his women fat and ugly like Antonia. That wasn't right. Robert didn't think her ugly. She turned in bed. What was Jane doing there? She should be with James. They were married now, she told the nurse.

"Congratulations," said the cool voice. "Drink this, Mrs Lambert."

"I'm not Mrs Lambert. I'm Antonia Blackberne now. Why should Jane get married before we did? She isn't pregnant."

"Not fair," the voice agreed. "Just lie quietly and you'll be fine."

"How's the induction going?" said a male voice.

"Fine. Is her husband here yet?"

"Robert? I want Robert," Antonia shouted.

"He'll be here. Just another prick in the arm and you may feel a few more contractions."

Antonia tried to scratch her head but her hands felt like bunches of bananas and the backache came and went in waves. "Something for my back?" she asked.

"In a little while," the nurse said and walked away, merging with the other movements in the room and the sound of a male voice again, outside the room this time and muted by the almost closed door.

"Don't talk to her yet. Wait until she is well on in labour and then you can be useful," the nurse said. "At this moment she is confused." Her voice was softer now with a smile in it.

Antonia smiled too. Robert had that effect on women.

"Let me tie your mask," the nurse said. "I can see that you are not at home in these places."

"What a nerve," Antonia murmured, but relaxed. The nurse was human after all and was trying to help Robert. Poor dear, he'll be all fingers and thumbs trying to get into a gown and mask.

"I have to take a sample of your blood," the sister said. "Nurse, fetch a syringe tray." There was a masculine murmur of dissent. "It's for cross-matching before the baby comes, in case he or she needs it, and a father can often give some. Yes, there has been a snag or two but we have everything under control now."

The rest was lost as the first sharp pain came low in her belly and when Antonia listened again she heard the nurse explaining that even a father's blood might be incompatible, but it was essential to know what was available before they rushed a supply from the blood bank. The woman was a natural for advertising, Antonia thought, and concentrated on her relaxation during the next contraction now that she knew Robert was close by.

"Is it next week already?" she asked owlishly. "What I mean is that I am not due yet for a week or so. If Robert is here he can take me home to wait there."

"We'll talk about it later. Now just think about those contractions. Can you hear me, Antonia? Breathe deeply as they taught you in class and you will soon have your baby, a bit early but we think it's best to bring it on now as you do have headaches. That's right. Good girl!"

Waves of something that seemed about to be pain came and went as she breathed in gas and air. She was tense and uncomfortable and then free and floating on the edge of comfort again and again. Someone screamed but she was too busy to know that it was her own cry. Between the waves she was calm and the beating in her head was not so bad. The pattern changed and she wanted to push the baby out, to finish with it and get some sleep. "I want Robert," she called. "Robert!" She was flooded with loneliness.

"Stand over there and hold her hand," a voice said. "It's all right. Your husband is here."

"Robert. My darling, I thought I'd lost you." Tears flowed down her face and her vision was blurred. Another contraction took all her strength and effort and she clung to the hand that took hers in a strong clasp. As the wave receded she opened her eyes wide and turned her head.

The eyes above the mask were cold and gave her no comfort. "Go away!" she screamed. "Get him out of here! I want Robert. I want my true husband, my lover, my companion – get me Robert. He's the father of my baby." She was hysterical. A hand tried to take Marcel's away from her but he brushed the nurse aside. The voice that had given so much ease and comfort now trembled and sounded shrill as the nurse tried to persuade him to leave the bedside.

Marcel took an even tighter grip, iron hard and hurting her swollen fingers.

"Mr Lambert, I must insist. You must go. I can't have my patient upset like this. I had no idea. Oh, can't you see that she is very ill and we have to get this baby out safely?"

"She's my wife and that's my baby," Marcel said savagely.

"Do you want to kill her?" The voice was curt and urgent.

There was a flurry of footsteps and a man's voice took over. "Get out," he orderd crisply. "What the hell do you think you are achieving by upsetting her?"

"I don't care about her! Just get my baby out and she can go to hell." Marcel's fingers dug into her wrist as the doctor tried to ease him away from the bed, and Antonia felt another deep contraction building up.

Granny had told her of old midwives who made their patients bite on a towel and to grip anything near to take away the pain. Antonia turned her head and buried her teeth into the hand that held her and it was wonderful to transfer the pain to him.

Warm blood oozed from his hand and he drew back sharply, letting go. Antonia wiped her mouth clean on the sheet as the contraction subsided and she was suddenly clear-minded. It was possible to work now and to get this over with no thought but for the primeval urge to have her baby, and half an hour afterwards, she heard the baby cry and felt a slippery mass being pushed gently into her arms.

"It's a girl; a lovely little girl," said Sister Granger. Antonia lay exhausted, watching the bag on the blood pressure cuff inflate. "Right," Sister said cheerfully. "It's going down already. Feeling better?"

"Yes." Miraculously, it was true. The heavy beat of her pulse was slackening and she was wide awake and very thirsty. "Can I have a drink?"

"Now you are delivered, you can. Don't overdo it for the next hour or so and when we take the next reading of your BP we should be able to give you more. It's amazing how quickly the blood pressure comes down once the baby is out."

Antonia frowned. The girl was too bright and chatty, as if she had something to hide. "What's wrong?"

"Nothing that a good sleep can't put right."

"The baby? You haven't let him take the baby?"

"Of course not!"

Antonia tried to sit up. "He has no right here. We are getting divorced. Where is Robert?"

"I'm terribly sorry about all this, Mrs Lambert."

"How did he know? And don't call me Mrs Lambert. I'm Antonia or Mrs Blackberne but *never* again that name."

"Your address book. You said your husband was away and Nurse rang the Lambert number."

"Does Robert know?" She struggled up again, her head throbbing. "Where is he?"

"He knows all about it and he's in the waiting room. He's fine now," she added.

"I want to see him and I want my baby."

"Soon. First, a nap."

Sleep and high places, the poet said. Sleep came swiftly after hands that turned her and cleaned her back and had put on fresh clothes and powdered her with sweet-smelling talc had become part of the dream. Raised voices were hurriedly shut out by the closing of a door.

Antonia woke to the sound of babies crying and somewhere in her breasts a pulse made her want to feed her baby. She struggled higher and saw a nurse watching her from a chair by the window. "Where's my baby?" she asked.

"The consultant is doing a round and he's in the nursery now."

"The others have their babies; I can hear them."

"Not the new deliveries," the nurse said firmly.

"Where's Robert? The baby's father?" Antonia was speaking quietly now and there could be no doubt that she was completely rational.

"Mrs Lambert—"

"Please don't call me that. If you can't use Robert's name, then I think I can legally call myself by my maiden name. The fact remains that Robert is the father of this child and I have the right to see him now." She looked at the girl, daring her to refuse. "I was told he is here."

The girl bit her lip, obviously too junior to cope with emotional crises. "I'll get Sister," she said, and fled.

Sister Granger looked as fresh and young as morning dew, but she stifled a yawn. "Did you sleep well?" she asked. "You look terrific."

"Not as terrific as I was," said Antonia, patting her concave abdomen. She examined her fingers. "They seem to get smaller each time I look at them. I feel tired but quite well and ready to see the baby and its father."

"He's with the doctor now." Sister Granger smiled. "You had loads of flowers from the university and from Robert, of course."

"This early? I suppose it isn't really early now."

"He must have telephoned just before he had to . . ."

"Before he had to what?"

Sister Granger sat on the bed. "Your baby had a very rough passage, but she's fine now. She was shocked at birth and

246

the placenta was impoverished because of your condition." Antonia twisted the sheet into a knot. "It's all right, I promise you," Sister went on seriously. "The baby will be fine but she needed a change of blood; a whole lot, to be exact, from a donor from the same group and compatibility."

"Robert?"

"Yes, it was a good thing that he arrived in time." Antonia sighed with relief. "I'm terribly sorry about the mix up of phone numbers, but as we had never met you or Robert or your husband and a man came and said we had sent for him and he was Mr Lambert, we took it for granted that he was the father." A hidden reproach was still there.

"Not your fault. We should have come to see you," Antonia admitted.

"I can see his point of view. He was very difficult but you *are* still married to him."

"Only for another week or so. Tell me about the baby."

"We took a specimen of blood from your . . . Mr Lambert and found we couldn't use his blood at all."

"Thank God!"

"He just wouldn't believe us. The doctor had to talk to him very firmly and told him that he had sent the rest of the blood for tests to see if he could be the father of the child." She tightened her lips. "He seemed so attractive when he first came here but after that he was very rude to everyone. You can go off people," she added with feeling.

"I know what you mean," Antonia said. "I hope you have convinced him that the baby has nothing to do with him?"

"I hinted that he could marry again and have more children, and he really frightened me. I thought he was going to hit me!" She looked at Antonia with unveiled curiosity. "Is it true, Antonia? He told the doctor that he couldn't have any children now. I can't see why this should be his only chance of a family. He's quite a dish and there must be many women who go for that type."

"Poor Marcel." For the first time, Antonia felt a tinge of sympathy for the man who had nearly wrecked her life. "It could be true. He was injured in a rock fall and had a bad infection which may have made him permanently sterile." She looked anxious. "I had hoped that he would marry a colleague who was with him in South America and have showers of beautiful babies and forget about this one."

Sister Granger took her hand. "We saw how important all this might be, so if it's any help, we now have the result of the paternity test and no way could he have fathered this baby. It is definite and will stand in a court of law if that ever becomes necessary."

"Bless you. Has he gone?" Antonia asked.

"Yes, he has. For a while, he watched the staff going in and out of the nursery and we wondered if he'd do something stupid, but he's gone now and I don't think he'll come back."

"Does he know that Robert gave blood?"

"Yes, he stayed until the procedure was over and asked if he could see the infant once before he left." Antonia caught her breath.

"It was quite safe. We kept him outside the big window

to the nursery and there were two male doctors and a nurse standing by."

"Did he say anything?"

"He looked shocked, as if he expected to see something quite different. He said something about the baby having no resemblance to you and had we made a mistake?" She glanced at Antonia's set face. "I was sorry for him. I think he wanted the baby to be like you, even if it wasn't his."

"We are both dark," said Antonia.

"I think it was then that he realised the baby had Robert's blood in more ways than one and that gave him first claim. It must have been very hard to take."

Sister Granger stood up and smoothed down her neat uniform dress. "He was wise to leave then with dignity. If he had managed to obtain custody he would have been haunted by you and Robert for ever."

"I must see her." The hunger for her child was overwhelming.

"Nurse, bring a wheelchair. Your baby will be in the nursery for a day or so just to be safe from infection, so don't be alarmed when you can only see her through glass. They finished the blood change and she's bathed and tidy and a good pink colour, so intensive care isn't necessary. I think you may be able to hold her tomorrow, but wheelchairs are not allowed in there."

Two gowned and masked figures stood by a cot. One of the men held a baby in his arms ready to show her through the window. Tears of love and laughter flowed down Antonia's cheeks. "It's ridiculous. They are so much alike," she said, although Robert was pale after giving blood, and the baby began to howl, making her face very red.

He handed the baby to the nurse with heartrending tenderness and came out to see her. He bent to kiss her and she buried her face in the white gown.

There was no time to think of Marcel now. "She may not be a boy but she certainly has a lot of my blood in her," Robert said with feeling, rubbing his sore arm. "We'll call her Roberta."

Antonia smiled. Roberta would soon lie in a pram and look up at the waving spring leaves of the poplars as they lulled her to sleep. "We needn't go to France," she said. "Can we go home soon? It looks as if I have to put up with two of a kind now."